North Morgan was born in 1980. In 2007, he created the fictional blog London Preppy, which has been featured in *Dazed & Confused*, *Time Out* and *Attitude* amongst other publications. London Preppy has been an international success, attracting over 1.5 million hits by the time North published his first short story as part of the *Boys & Girls* anthology, launched at the London Literature Festival in 2010. *Highlights of My Last Regret* is the highly anticipated sequel to his debut novel, *Exit Through The Wound*, which was published to critical acclaim in 2011.

He currently lives in California.

For more information visit:

northmorgan.com

D1667774

Also by North Morgan

EXIT THROUGH THE WOUND

HIGHLIGHTS OF MY LAST REGRET

North Morgan

LIMEHOUSE
BOOKS

For Peter

1

'Women are outrageously superficial,' I'm telling him.

'Look how they choose partners. In high school and college, every girl is after the jocks. They don't care how much of a dick a guy is, or how stupid, just as long as he's popular and good at sports.'

'You're *outraged* by that, are you?' Markus says.

His eyes are darting off everywhere around me and I'm surprised that he's even heard me. Ignoring him, I continue.

'When they hit their late 20s, everything changes. They want to find the nearest victim, marry him and settle down. And because of that, their priorities shift. Not towards anything of any substance, mind you. It's just that the most important factor is now financial success. All the guys know this, of course, so they give up on any pretenses they previously made of caring to look attractive, keep in shape and wear nice clothes. And all their efforts are concentrated towards one thing: making money.'

This appears to be of no interest to him, so Markus makes his way back into the house, walking past the bar that's set up by the pool area outside. I follow him. Inside, he starts going through the liquor cabinet in a small sitting room. We're the only people here. He picks up what looks like a bottle of old Scotch, fills the red cup he's been holding halfway to the top, takes a sip and swallows two pills. 'Do you want some?' he asks. I shake my head no.

'Of course. Parke Hudson doesn't drink or take drugs,' he says in a mock innocent voice.

Markus is a trust fund waste of space, and my closest friend.

On this warm evening in March, we're hanging out at a pool party in somebody's house in the Hollywood Hills, because hang out is what you have to do. I'm just back from driving Ryan to the airport. I dropped her off outside the terminal building, underneath a sign that said 'Arrivals'. She wanted to know why I was stopping there and where exactly Departures were – I told her to step inside the building and have a look around, I'm sure she would find it. I had a party to go back to. Ryan is the love of my life, this month. She's the woman I'll grow old with, this year. I tell her the first half of these sentences a few times a day.

On the way to the airport she told me that she's going to miss me, I teared up and told her the same, she said that she's been waiting for this all her life, I told her I never thought something so wonderful would happen, I never expected this. She said our relationship is perfect, we belong to each other, I told her we're one, nothing will tear us apart. I said these exact words, or many, many other words to the same effect. Back at the party, it's 11pm, midnight, 1am on this Saturday night and I'm surrounded by people who are shamefully high or drunk; a shame they cannot currently feel. Most of the guests have been here partying since Friday evening. Ryan and I came over earlier this afternoon, but she had to leave early to catch a flight to Albuquerque where she's going to spend the next few days with her family.

Markus was one of the first people here yesterday. Just so I can judge him, I ask him what he has taken in the space of the last eighteen hours or so. He's unable to formulate lists in his head at this point, but the list that he needs to make would include: four Ecstasy, lines of coke not adding up to a gram but not far off, one MDMA capsule, two Adderall, and several alcoholic drinks (Scotch, some Mai Tais they were serving earlier). I haven't taken anything, because I never do.

We're now walking around with Markus looking for the next free hit from someone or the next person he wants to talk to. As it happens the two are never combined. There are nearly one hundred people in the house, hiding in rooms, splayed on couches, sharing showers, throwing each other in the pool, trying on sunglasses, smoking pot, swapping swimwear, crushing pills, embracing in beds, taking pictures, dancing, shuffling, fucking, snorting.

I see Katie. She is tall, slim, and toned in a way that makes you think she can't hold a real job (what would people think if they had to share an office with her?), more attractive than any other girl at this house. This is no mean feat for a springtime pool party in the Hollywood Hills.

I sort of know her and she sort of knows me, although we've never actually spoken to each other, so I leave Markus talking to some annoying gay kid who must have a pocketful of drugs, go up to her and introduce myself. She repeats my name three times, without giving me hers. This is her state of mind. Everyone at this party is completely wasted, I'm thinking. Katie's wearing a white tank top and yellow bikini bottoms and nothing else. A few minutes into our one-sided conversation, which involves me attempting some innocuous statements about how fun this party is and her smiling at me moronically with eyes that can't focus, I grab my phone, pull the front of her tank top out and take a take a picture of her – admittedly, quite small – breasts from above. She laughs and pushes me away, with a hand that's actually gripping my shirt, not letting go, so I do it again. This time, she asks to take a look at the pictures and deletes the worst one. This is quite impressive, as at least it indicates that she's able to connect with her surroundings enough to do *something*.

I spot my friend Jeremy Thibeaux sitting in the hot tub with a couple of not very attractive girls that I don't recognize, and raise my arm to get his attention. When he looks over, I point down at Katie and signal that we're coming over. It's not very difficult to drag her down to the back of the garden, where the hot tub is. I take my shirt and pants off, pick up Katie and playfully throw her in, which she takes as her cue to let out a scream. The two other girls, annoyed, climb out and I step in, wearing just my underwear, to take their spaces with Katie. Her white tank is soaked and has turned completely see-through. She's sitting between Jeremy and me, with her right leg touching my left, as Jeremy correctly interprets my stare and decides to leave. He climbs out and walks back to the main party, possibly to try and finish off whatever he had started with those two girls. Katie, seemingly awakened slightly by having been thrown into a mass of water, decides to take these rare moments of lucidness and share a personal story. She asks if I know this girl called Rae Prinz, who's also at this party, and unfortunately I do. Rae is one of a number of worthless, Hollywood-based socialite wannabes, whose priorities are to maintain an all-season tan and fuck as many models/actors as possible. A resounding 7 out of 10 – both facially and body-wise – she stands out as being one of the most shallow of her demographic group and exclusively surrounds herself with girls she considers to be less attractive, in order to enhance her messed up self esteem. She recently got engaged to Tommy Gillman, a film industry also-ran who's podgy and not even that rich, for Christ's sake. Though I guess she's been smart enough to grab the first guy who's substandard and insecure enough to treat her like a princess. I was there the night when Tommy proposed to Rae. It was her birthday party at this house they had rented for the weekend down in Palm Springs, and she emerged at some point flashing an adequate, if not extravagant, ring with a love-struck look on her face. The love was directed at the ring rather than the person who offered it, this much was quite obvious. Later on the same night and as I was fucking Ryan in one of the bathrooms, Tommy and Rae walked in requesting a foursome – we said no – an incident that doesn't fill me with confidence that this will be a successful marriage, if it ever materializes.

Knowing Rae and being aware of what Katie looks like, I can see where this is going.

'Yes, I think I've heard of her,' I say. 'Go on, what mean-spirited comment did she make?'

'Ha. How do you know this? You're so clever, Parke.'

She giggles in a girly manner, which I find gross and attractive, and continues.

'You see, I was sitting on the side of the pool earlier sipping my drink and she came and sat next to me. I'd only spoken to her, like, once or twice before. So she says to me, she says, "Katie, you're so pretty. There isn't a single guy in this house who hasn't noticed you. So don't take what I'm about to tell you the wrong way."'

'Oh God,' I say.

'I know, right? So she says to me: "Again, please don't think I'm criticizing you. I had the same issue and it was really knocking my confidence. But don't let it worry you. You know that a boob job is literally, like, the most risk-free procedure you can ever have done. I can give you the name of the guy that did mine." Can you *believe* her?'

I'm slightly stunned, although this does sound completely in character. 'Jesus. What did you say?' I ask.

Katie looks sufficiently upset, more so than angry, and remains quiet. I'm actually feeling a little sad for her.

'Listen, Katie. You can't take people like Rae seriously. There's nothing that causes instant, unjustified aggravation like physical beauty does. And you really are a beautiful girl.'

She whispers 'Thank you' and I lean into her. I kiss her on the lips, with both my hands on the back of her head, stroking her hair. She kisses me back, holding my shoulders, the back of my neck, pushing my face harder into hers. Her sadness is gone. I'm kissing her open mouth, the bitchy girl that made her feel momentarily awful somewhere in the house, maybe in the pool, the girl that I'm dating lost in the desert near Albuquerque, with her family somewhere, nowhere on my mind, I feel high even though I'm completely sober, I feel fucking amazing, this is my life, I'm kissing her more, I'm coming up, I'm coming up, I'm coming up.

It takes only a few minutes to come back to my senses and wonder why I'm doing this. Starting to feel sorry for Ryan – perhaps I've underestimated my feelings for her – I pull away, mutter a quick apology to Katie mentioning something about having a girlfriend and hurriedly get out of the hot tub. I grab a towel from the poolside, wrap it round my waist and walk inside the house, upstairs, where I find an empty bathroom and dry myself. I quickly jerk off, my brief orgasm marred by regret, and go out naked. The next room that I walk in has one of those tasteless gas log fireplaces, which is lit (despite the warm weather and the air conditioning also being on), so I hang my wet underwear next to it to dry and lie down on the couch opposite. There's also a bed in the room and I can make out the silhouettes of two people sleeping in it. I can't tell who they are and whether I know them. The windows are open, and I can hear the music loudly from the party, still going strong downstairs, but I can usually sleep through anything and I quickly nod off.

When Ryan calls me the next evening, I'm still at the party. There seems to be a rotating cast of guests who've kept the place busy all through Sunday as well, although it's now down to just 10-15 people. I didn't have anywhere else I particularly wanted to go, so I stayed here after waking up around noon. I still don't know whose house this is.

My phone rings when I'm in the middle of a water pistol fight with Markus, plus two girls and another guy, all of whom I've just met. We've all got feathered Indian headdresses on that somebody brought and left here at some point during the weekend. Markus, the girls and I are all wearing swimsuits and the third guy is wearing only a jockstrap.

'Hello, my love,' I say, answering the phone.

'Hi. I miss you. How's your Sunday?'

'It's been pretty cool. I'm hungry though, I think they've run out of food.'

'Wait. You're still there?'

'Well, yes. Markus's here too. We've been hanging out. He says hi.'

There's an awkward, dissatisfied pause, which I should have expected.

'Did you have sex with anyone?'

'Ry. Of course I didn't have sex with anyone. I love you, baby.'

Another pause.

'Did you kiss anyone?'

How the fuck does she know?

I try to weigh my options and decide what the least damaging thing is to say. In the time that it takes me to do this, she's already interpreted my silence.

'Well?'

I think it's too late to lie, so I say:

'I had a quick kiss with Katie; you don't mind that, do you?'

It seems that she does, because she calls me a fucking jerk and hangs up. Immediately, she calls back sounding tearful and asks for details of how it happened. I give most of the story, repeat several times that we did nothing more than share a quick kiss, tell her to stop crying, tear up because I'm not great under pressure and promise to leave the party immediately. When she's decided that we've exhausted the subject and we hang up, I dive into the pool to cover up the fact that I'm flustered and my eyes are red, refill my pistol and go back to my game. Jockstrap guy and Markus have chased one of the two girls into the living room and are aggressively squirting water all over her. She's trapped in a corner between two full-length wall mirrors. All four of them, including the second girl who's taking a movie of this on her phone, are laughing hysterically. I shoot a large stream of water straight in her face causing her to lose her grip and drop the phone on the marble floor. The screen cracks on impact, but remains in place. She picks the phone up and points it back at the girl in the corner, who's now down on her knees.

2

I finally make it back to my place around 4am on Monday morning. The last few people at the party were sitting there getting stoned in a big circle of jerks, which turned out to be a blessing for me, as I was finally bored enough to get out of there. Without ever drinking or taking drugs, hanging out around people who are high on uppers like Ecstasy or cocaine is tolerable, if I'm in the right frame of mind. Drunk people I just want to kill, so that also provides some social thrills I suppose, but people who are stoned are pretty fucking intolerable and absolutely no fun to be around.

I live in a building in Westwood, on the same floor as Markus, who actually found the apartment for me when I moved over to LA last summer. Our apartments are identical, right next to each other, although he owns his and I'm renting mine. I last sent a text to Ryan a few hours ago and told her I was now home. She hasn't replied, which upsets me a little, but I don't think I should call her or even text again, since it's the middle of the night even in Albuquerque, which sounds like should be in a completely different time zone, perhaps on a different continent, and she'll probably know I was lying before. Well, I'm sure she knows. She'll just have confirmation. I sit down in my office with a bowl of cereal and start reading one of numerous bookmarked conspiracy theory websites about the 1932 Lindbergh baby kidnapping until I'm too tired to keep my eyes open. When I look at the clock, the time is 4.44am. This being a great sign – four has always been my favorite number – I go to bed. I went through a phase when I was very young and had developed a minor obsessive-compulsive habit of doing everything four times, in order to put my mind at ease about impending dangers, bad fortune and general adversity. I guess it made sense for a short while that if I turned the light on and off four times each time I entered a room, I would be safe from harm; temporarily anyway. This was a foolish habit, I was well aware of that, but I didn't mind it too much, it wasn't that disruptive. There came a point a few years ago, however, when 'having OCD' was one of a number of minor psychological disturbances that every attention-seeking dullard claimed for themselves when attempting to generate some interest in their poor self. Others conditions on that list included ADD (also ADHD for those who'd spend more than two minutes online shopping for 'cool' disorders), mild depressions, suffering panic attacks, and 'being dead inside'. When I became aware of that (the fact that being psychologically undamaged was actually more rare than claiming to have some made-up First World disorder) I focused all my strength on getting over this shortcoming. Actually, getting over myself. This has taken the best part of the last decade, but right now, whenever I get a slight urge for a perfectly symmetrical repetition of any action in quadruple sequence, well, I take a mental step back (emphasis on mental) and try to convince myself that I'm a different person, a person that doesn't have any obsessive-compulsive needs to do anything like that, because he's balanced, in control, uncomplicated. This technique seems to work for me and I'm sticking with it.

It's just before noon when I wake up. I check my phone and various email accounts immediately, but Ryan still hasn't got in touch. I give her a call, which goes unanswered. She is now beginning to really piss me off.

It's too late to go into the office – I can always do some work from home later – so I have some breakfast and decide to go next-door and annoy Markus. He might have some ridiculous relationship tips to give me that might prove to be useful by a fluke. I let myself in using my key and go straight into his bedroom. It's only early afternoon on a Monday, so it makes total sense that he would still be asleep. I pull the curtains open all the way, happy for the bright sunlight coming in from the full-length windows facing the pool outside to abruptly wake him up. He grunts and covers his head with a pillow, so I pull his cover and tell him that we're facing some very serious problems and he needs to wake up. I can't even begin to imagine what violent combinations of hangovers and comedowns he's currently suffering, deeming him unresponsive, so I switch on his stereo and start blasting some of the noise crap he listens to throughout the apartment. I'm not being dismissive – the genre of music he favors is categorized as 'noise'. This is all the indication that anyone needs in order to assess what's going on inside this person's head, to be honest. He is somebody whose favorite type of music includes the subgenre 'cacophony'. I exit the room taking the remote control with me, which means that he has to get up to make it stop, even though listening to this blasting through the apartment I don't know which one of us I'm really punishing. Feeling particularly amiable (as well as wanting to get him into awake, conversational mode more quickly) I make him a cup of coffee and put some aspirin next to a glass of water. I sit on a stool in the open plan kitchen, a kitchen that's unfortunately exactly the same as mine in these ultra-modern apartments, which I kinda loathe, and wait for him. Only when he's sat opposite me sipping his coffee and attempting to make me drop dead with his stare, do I turn the music down.

'So she's ignoring you, I take it?' he says.

Markus looks like a crazed Nazi homosexual, on first impressions at least. He's not actually gay, but is a prime specimen of what might have offensively been referred to as the Aryan race: tall, brawny, with cropped yellow hair that shines white under the sun, a slender pointed nose and intense green eyes, all enhanced by a Californian tan. Upon first seeing him, you can't help but think of hundreds of extras cast in the previous century to play young members of Hitler's Wehrmacht in terrifying films dramatizing the war. The type that looks so restrained, obedient and single-mindedly dedicated to this absurd vision shared by other men who look exactly like him that you think there must be a sexual incentive there, there's no other way. Markus is anything but restrained and obedient, of course, but aesthetically he's right up there. As for the Nazi connection, this is pure speculation and I have no further evidence apart from his surname being Brandt and the fact that his family is the richest I know other than mine (if a handful of people who are biologically connected but never see, interact with or care for each other can be classified as a family). They moved over from Europe some seventy years ago and nobody exactly knows where all this money came from.

People have actually always mistaken us for brothers, although I'm a couple of inches shorter and my hair is more sandy blonde than Nazi yellow, which gives me a less severe look. At 24, Markus is one year older than me and I've known him all my life. We both grew up in Hillsborough, just south of San Francisco, and spent our early developing years bonding over not only being physically alike, but also almost universally hated at the schools we went to whilst growing up. Because the greatest sin you can commit in those types of schools – second only to coming from a poor family and attending on some sort of humiliating scholarship – is coming from the family that is the richest.

'I don't know why you bother,' Markus continues.

'I bother because I love her.'

'Oh. Well this seems to be a new ability you've developed there. Loving human beings other than yourself.'

'That's funny. I do love her.'

'You like her at the very most. She's pretty enough for you to want to be seen with her and for some reason, which is unclear to me still, you're obsessed with the idea of having a girlfriend at the moment.'

'That's a lot of insight from somebody who's just woken up and is probably still drunk and high.'

'You shouldn't have dragged me out of bed if you don't want to hear my insight. I can easily go back if you like. In any case, I'm just saying. If you do love Ryan you probably shouldn't be making out with random girls at parties, should you? What's her name again?'

'Katie.'

'Of course, Katie. She's hot. She models, doesn't she? Seems like quite the achiever.'

'It's more work than you've ever done in your life.'

'Let's Google her.'

'No Markus, let's not.'

He pulls out his iPad and asks for a last name. I don't actually know this, but I remember she mentioned having just done a big job with Adidas, so after a couple more minutes of pretending I don't want to look her up, I tell him to look for that.

He opens adidas.com and looks around the website for a while, but all we can see are pictures of sportswear – strap tops, graphic tees, track tops, tights and even bikinis all filled up as if a person is wearing them, but actually floating in mid-air with no one inside.

'Which one is she?' Markus asks.

'She's inside each and every one of these.'

'You can totally tell it's her,' Markus says.

'Yes, I'd recognize her spirit anywhere.'

He goes on Google and types in 'Adidas commercial 2012' and we finally get a result. There are two clips on YouTube uploaded by Adidas within the last six months with 20,000-30,000 views each, starring Katie in all her sportswear glory. They're a couple of minutes long each and we watch them both silently, transfixed. Katie sitting on a sidewalk tying up her shoelaces, Katie going up and down metal stairs in a disused industrial-looking building, Katie on a rooftop at night pensively looking over downtown LA, Katie running through an abandoned meat market, Katie against a cement wall pointlessly changing between hooded tops and pairs of sneakers then walking away leaving her old clothes behind, Katie jogging across the wet ground in an open-air parking garage in early dawn, Katie sitting down on some rail tracks with complete disregard for her personal safety, all the scenes played to a highly dramatic instrumental soundtrack with strings and booming drums.

'This is really fantastic work. For the first time in my adult life, I think I could really use a drink right now,' I comment.

'Yes, she must be very pleased with herself. Does she actually live on the streets, because if not, she is really an amazing actor. Both videos were full of suspense, I never knew what she was going to do or wear next.'

'And you should have fucked her,' he adds.

'No, I shouldn't,' I almost shout at him. 'Stop saying that, and let's stop talking about Katie. She's not helping with my problem. In fact, she's the cause of my problem.'

'I'm sure you used to be fun at some point. Anyway. Try calling Ryan now. See if she picks up.'

'She won't,' I say and give her another missed call. 'See?'

'Where is she? At work?'

'No, remember? She's gone to see her family in Albuquerque.'

'Albuh-what?'

'Albuquerque.'

'What-uquerque?'

'Shut up. Why do you find it hilarious that somebody would be from a small town in a fifth-rate State?' I'm a complete hypocrite when I talk to Markus, obviously.

'For the same reasons that you do. How long is she there for?'

'I think until next Sunday. There's a cousin's wedding this weekend or something. She'd asked me to go, but I wasn't feeling suicidal at the time.'

'Oh my God, go. You have to go. Imagine. You turn up, surprise her, spend quality time with the in-laws, bond with her buck-toothed cousins on a fishing trip in the Albuquerque river, she's bound to forgive you ... if that's what you want.'

'There's no Albuquerque river.'

'So you're going?'

I glance at my phone, which remains silent, and take a deep breath because I feel that it suits the moment. 'Yes, I'll go. I thought about this before you suggested it, by the way. This is not *your* idea.'

'Oh I'm sure. Go pack for your trip now, while I go back to bed for a bit. There's no time to waste, the sooner you get there, the better. Ryan must be getting angrier by the minute and I don't have any projects for this week; I need the updates.'

'Don't worry, I'll be reporting back on everything.'

'Awesome. This is going to be fun. Are you nervous about meeting the in-laws? What's your approach going to be?'

'Um, no I'm not nervous. This isn't a conventional 'meet the parents' situation, is it? I'm not trying to gain *their* approval. After all, I'm the one with money and from a higher social class. They should be worried instead.'

'Fair enough. Just be polite, I guess. Try not to give away the fact that you feel only contempt and boredom.'

'You may find this hard to believe, but this is my main failing when I've met people like that before. I sometimes comes across as stuck up and disdainful, apparently?'

'You're right. This, I just refuse to believe.'

3

I get to the airport just after 4pm and buy a ticket to Albuquerque, New Mexico. It seems a little unlikely that anyone would ever want to go there, but I mustn't know people very well, because there are ten flights a day from LAX and the next one I can catch leaves at 5.05pm. From my gate I call Ryan once again and she finally answers. She gives me a few lines about not being angry at me, just really, really, really disappointed, but I actually feel bad about what I did and don't even let the triteness of all this put me off (even though I still think she should practice some better, less predictable lines in the future). I apologize for the twelfth time since Sunday, tell her that I'm about to go have dinner with Markus and hang up. She calls me right back and asks whether I went to work today, which I think is a further attempt to point out how inadequate I am, so I lie to her that I did, resisting a sudden urge to abandon this stupid groveling trip I'm about to make, and board my plane.

I've never been to New Mexico, let alone Albuquerque, let alone the small town called Thoreau where her parents live. I've never met them in person before, but I certainly know a lot about them – I've even spoken to her mom on Skype a few times with Ryan during the last year, especially after we moved to LA. Thoreau is where she grew up before making her inevitable escape when she was 18. She chose Boston. We met there approximately twelve months ago while I was finishing the fourth year of my Computer Science degree at Harvard, having also moved east for college. Ryan graduated a few years back from Boston University and has fulfilled the potential of a precocious youth, when she stood out as extraordinarily gifted both in the state schools that she attended (though I can't imagine that sort of thing being too difficult) and amongst an immediate family with a ranching background (ditto). With the annoying added characteristics of being driven and hard-working, which I suppose come from growing up in an environment that you're desperate to disassociate yourself with and move away from, she's managed to advance both career and status-wise to a level that you think this is a woman who's never eaten meat from a cow that was butchered mere yards from the kitchen table.

Against expectations and as a shock even to myself, these are all reasons why I actually like this person and want to be with her. This is mostly surprising knowing my previous dating track record, which almost exclusively incorporated the frivolous, perky and shallow. OK, this might not be very fair, there are some smart girls at Harvard after all, but there hasn't been anyone as distinguished, refined, or even as complex as Ryan. I'd never thought I appreciated upward social adjustment this much, but I guess there are some people who perform it better than others. In terms of standing out from every other girl I've ever gone out with, I also need to make reference to Ryan's age. Five and a half years older than me, now at 28, she seems to have both more patience and less time for bullshit at the same time. It's an unusual combination that you don't come across in your average 20 year old. I think these personality traits are the reason why she's got so mad at me about this whole Katie thing. On the one hand she fully understands the situation and is ready to make allowances for dating somebody younger, with less life experience than her, but on the other hand there are certain indiscretions that she just finds unacceptable. And even though it makes my life more difficult on certain occasions, I guess I respect that. Perhaps I do want to be more responsible, after all.

On board this flight, I am able to successfully populate a list of the Top 5 women I'd have sex with (even discounting cabin crew members) which is pretty good going for a Monday evening flight to New Mexico that's not nearly full, and a short couple of hours later I'm in Albuquerque. My first thought is that it's not as hot as I'd expected it to be. Saying that, it's now 8pm here, and the sun has just gone down. I don't actually have an address for Ryan's parents' house, but I should be able to track her cell phone thanks to an app we have both downloaded on her insistence, so she can know all of my moves, all of the time without the need to ask me. This is the first instance when I will have been able to use this app to my advantage, rather than falling victim to the close scrutiny it provides. She's not always been successful though – soon after we got this app, I coincidentally experienced the onset of a form of early dementia, causing me to constantly misplace my handset, leave it at work, etc. Conversely,

I shouldn't have any problems locating Ryan through her cell phone at all. She's usually attached to it, so I'm going to have to just make my way to the green dot on my screen. I'm guessing her phone is probably in her back pocket waiting to ignore my calls. Google Maps tells me that it's a two-and-a-half-hour drive from the airport to the particular part of wilderness that these people call home and I can't pretend that a four-and-a-half-hour journey in total doesn't make me think this was perhaps too much effort, but I'm here now and have no option but to go.

I'm driving my rental car in silence, at a speed that indicates I don't really want to get there very soon, and I'm trying to take in the surroundings, imagine what it's like to call this place your home, to know this is where you come from, where your ties are. I'm trying to think why I've never felt inclined to visit before and why I'm here now. I think in the year that we've dated, Ryan's been back maybe two or three times. It seems like an awful waste of someone's already limited vacation time, and I'm actually pretty sure that she hates it, but there must be some sort of attachment that keeps her coming back. I've been back to San Francisco to visit my mother much more often than that, but I don't really have a job where I necessarily need to be physically, and at the end of the day I'm proud to be where I'm from. I don't know, maybe they're blackmailing her or something.

I know that her ex boyfriend, Trevor, came over with her and visited a lot. But that's a whole different messed up story. Even thinking about him now sort of makes me angry: how she chose to go out with him, how she stayed with him for so long, and how she put up with everything. It also makes me think that whatever I do, well, I can't be as useless. They met when she was in the last semester of her LLM in American Law at Boston University, at a time when Ryan had fallen into a very familiar state of extreme anxiety and lack of confidence. A state, which, I've come to realize, has been underlying through her whole life. At this point it was related to finishing college, where she had done very well indeed, and worrying that this was her high point and that she wouldn't be able to make it in the real world. From what I've discussed with her – because I like to probe – and from my own personal prejudices and judgments, these sentiments of uncertainty were echoed by her family back in New Mexico, who routinely expressed that she wouldn't amount to anything and that she wasn't fooling anyone with her new life on the East Coast.

This was great timing for Trevor who at that time must have been looking for a new romantic project to get involved with, and by that I mean somebody new to latch on to and suck the life out of. He's eight years older than Ryan (though half as mature) so he'd just turned 30 when they first started dating. I came across the guy a couple of times in Boston and I've seen many pictures of him from when they were going out and he looks all right, I guess, nothing spectacular; a little malnourished, if anything. He's most definitely not worthy of the beauty of Ryan, of her immodest full mouth, her sparsely freckled cheekbones, her inattentive blue eyes that make you strive to keep her interest. But this was never about looks. Trevor's appeal, his way of infiltrating girls' minds, disgusting as this thought might be, was based on an artistic, free-spirited charm, that of a painter who doesn't have a talent to paint, nor the inclination to actually chase any of his half-assed dreams. I'll never really understand it, but some girls fall for that appalling type.

In any case, whatever it is that brought them together to begin with, five years into a relationship that was knocking her confidence even more – despite her advancing career as a paralegal in Boston – and becoming progressively more embittered she somehow found the strength to end it. I met her out in a bar just a couple of weeks after it had come to a final, massive blow following a prolonged break-up period. I like to think that I was the antithesis of everything Trevor represented, and she was ready to move on.

It's now just before 10.30pm and I've been in the car for over two hours. I've been driving across a dry, deserted landscape surrounded by nothing for the last hour or so, occasionally passing through small nowhere towns built on either side of the highway. Those are indicated by clusters of low, adobe-made buildings housing takeout restaurants, small-time lawyer offices, nail salons, and tattoo parlors. According to my iPhone I'm now very near to the point where it's tracking Ryan's cell. I have disabled sharing my location to avoid her looking me up and ruining the surprise. This current row of buildings must indicate Thoreau. I turn north off the highway following a road, which is starting to look more residential. There's a lot of ranch around. My phone leads me outside a drive, blocked by a disheveled wooden door, which at some point might have been painted white. I can see an old two-story house just a few yards away, but all the lights are off and the only sign of life is a dog, matching the fence in the way they have both seen better days, making his way to the bottom of the drive. I get out of the car. It's all so quiet. The dog sniffs my hand through the fence in a disinterested way and decides to lie down. I look at the time. It's 10.42pm, but it feels like 3am at least. I've got to let Ryan know that I'm here, I can't just drive into a house where everyone's asleep, even though I see that the gate is not locked and nothing would stop me.

I send a tentative text. I wait for a minute or two with no answer and give her a call. It rings out to voicemail. What if she's asleep and doesn't see my call until the morning? What if she's ignoring me again? Fuck, fuck, fuck, what if I have to spend the night in some horrifying motel in fucking rural New Mexico? As I'm starting to panic, she calls me back.

'Hey,' she says quietly. 'What's up?'

'I'm here.' I don't even want to play any games and have her guessing right now. I want to get instant credit for making this trip.

'Where's here?'

'I'm outside your house. Come meet me. Were you asleep? Are your parents asleep?'

'What? You're in Thoreau?'

'Yes, yes, yes. I'm sorry for everything that happened. I love you. I just got a flight here. Come meet me, please. Your dog seems to like me.'

'You…are…? How did you know where…? Oh never mind. You drove here from the airport, I assume? Leave your car outside, everyone's asleep. Just come to the front door, the gate is open. I'll meet you there.'

I park the car out of the way, I'm not sure it matters where exactly anyway, and walk through the wooden gate up the drive, shining an iPhone app flashlight, so I can see where I'm going. The dog is following me quietly. The front door opens and I see Ryan's silhouette standing there. She doesn't turn on any lights. I hug her tightly and kiss her nose, lips and cheeks, which feel wet with warm tears. I tell her that I love her more than life – seems appropriate for this moment – and she whispers 'I love you the same'. She takes my hand and leads me up the stairs, in a room at the back of the house. When we climb into bed, I ask: 'Are your parents asleep?' She puts her finger on my lips to silence me and nods yes.

I turn her body around so that she's lying in front of me facing away and move my hand down her stomach, as I start kissing her neck. She turns to me and mouths a very determined 'No'. I ignore this and start kissing her mouth. 'I'm going to fuck you'. She tries to pull away, but the fear in her eyes, the fear that she's about to get fucked with her parents asleep next door is turning me on, and I pull her back, pushing her pelvis into my hard-on. I don't understand her objection anyway. I can't imagine she hasn't done this before with Trevor. He's been here several times and he's clearly quite sick, plus I haven't heard any objections about me spending the night in her room. Her parents must be used to it. I pull her panties down. She seems to be resigned to it now and is kissing me back. Still on our sides, and with one hand around her neck touching her breasts, I use the other to spread her ass, before licking my fingers and sticking my middle, then index as well inside her rear hole. I sit up and pull her up from the waist onto all fours. I spit on my hand to lubricate my dick then slowly insert it into her ass. My right hand is covering her mouth drowning out sharp, agonizing grunts. I shoot my load inside her after a small warning and lie down on my back. I'm asleep very soon after.

4

I don't know exactly what time it is when Ryan climbs over me to get up, but I've got a very strong feeling it's nowhere near the right time for me to leave this bed. I lean down and look at my phone, which desperately needs charging, and drop it back on the floor aghast when I see the first two digits of the clock display: '05'. She must be mad. They must be mad. I let Ryan go wherever she feels that she needs to go at this ungodly hour and fall back to sleep grateful for the additional bed space. Is this what will be happening while I stay here? Did I not think this through?

I'm still alone in the room when I finally wake up. My phone is now completely dead and there's no clock around, but the sun is bright and warm and it looks like it could be late enough in the day to get up. I wish I knew how to tell exactly what time it is just by looking at the position of the sun in the sky, but unfortunately I didn't grow up on a farm. I'm sure there must be somebody around here who can teach me. Perhaps I can do that this week. I walk downstairs hoping not to cross paths with anyone yet and quietly pace through the living room to the front door. I can hear voices coming from the next room (I'm guessing the kitchen) – Ryan's being one of them – but that door is half-closed and whoever's in there can't see met yet. The room that I'm walking through is very large with a high ceiling and is painted white apart from one garish maroon wall, which I think is an unsuccessful approximation of an old estate house feel, failing due to the particular shade of maroon used, not to mention the overall surroundings and the zip code that we're in.

I walk out to the car to collect the bag that I've brought with me and when I get back into the house the damn dog crawls out of the kitchen and barks at me twice. This results in Ryan and her mom coming out to greet me enthusiastically, while all I want to do is go and brush my teeth. Saying that, I actually quite like Ryan's mom. Or what I know of Ryan's mom anyway. She's as friendly and warm as you imagine these country people to be, and in real life a little taller than I expected too. Her dad is supposedly this gruff, salt-of-the-earth type, so I will definitely be avoiding him, but the highlight of the family is Ben, an older brother of around 32, who's Thoreau through and through.

From all the stories I've half-listened to over the past year, after having an impossibly hard time finishing high school – through a combination of inherent stupidity and his favorite pastime being sniffing household cleaning products – he was given a menial job, out of pity, at the ranch where Ryan's dad has been working most of his life. This, however, also proved a task too far and he spent most of his 20s dropping in and out of employment and, consequently, society overall. Through this time he was financially supported by Ryan's parents, who, I'm assuming, begrudgingly were forced to share their already pretty meager income. Still, I definitely identify the presence of a soft spot, because I don't recall any stories of cutting him off or kicking him out, as these white trash families are prone to do when their offspring, unsurprisingly, turn out to be utterly inept no-hopers.

A few years ago, some poor local girl, who must have had a crushingly low sense of self-worth, fell in love with him and they ended up marrying. According to Ryan, who always puts on her rose-tinted glasses when she talks about Ben, this girl helped him become a new person, and with a revived sense of responsibility that came out of nowhere he returned to the ranch job and has managed to keep it consistently and successfully for the biggest part of the last couple of years. It sometimes feels like she's talking about a recovering meth addict when she tells his story. 'Oh yes, Ben is doing really great. He hasn't missed work for months now.' Where 'missed work' stands for 'used crystal meth'. Unfortunately though, I'm a cynical person and I know very well what happens in the long term both to people like Ben and deceitful drug addicts. Nonetheless, these are views that I avoid discussing with Ryan, partly because I want to be nice and partly because I don't really care. So when she last mentioned them a few months ago, painting an inconceivably temperate alternate reality of them living in the next town along with Ben working at the ranch, his wife doing her pedestrian secretarial job at this real estate place in Albuquerque, both absorbed in their domestic bliss along with their 14-month-old infant, I kept quiet. Why bother? If anything, this will serve me well on this visit now, as I won't even have to see him much.

As it happens of course, next thing I know, a pale, somewhat overweight man with severe acne scars on his bloated, unshaved faced is coming down the stairs. Wearing just a pair of crummy plaid boxer shorts, he walks straight into the kitchen ignoring all three of us, now sitting around the old dining table in the main room. Ben.

I widen my eyes in Ryan's direction, Ryan starts eyeballing the ceiling fan wishing I had never come, and Ryan's mom bites her lip and suddenly remembers she needs to check on the baby. What fucking baby? When she's gone back into the kitchen, we head out to the porch and sit on an old, wooden swing hanging from the ceiling on four thick, rusty chains. The whole thing creaks every time I breathe. I'm trying to prevent the fact that I still haven't brushed my teeth from burning a visible hole into my skull, by concentrating on something else. There are lots of stimuli around. I pick two bunches of dried chili peppers also hanging at the porch, both about half as tall as I am. I've never seen this before.

'That's Ben, right? Isn't he working today?' I ask.

'He hasn't worked for a couple of months. He's been having some problems.'

No fucking kidding, I think. 'Oh. Sorry to hear that. What's wrong?' I say.

'I don't know why I'm telling you this, because you're only going to make fun of everything, like you always do.'

'You're telling me this because I'm here and staying for five days and he's clearly moved back in and he's more useless than ever and he's going to be in my face for the rest of the week and you can't hide it anymore.'

'Don't say that. I really wouldn't.'

'Well, the thing is that he had an affair and Jen found out about it and asked him to move out. And she doesn't want to talk to him and he's feeling depressed about the whole thing. She wouldn't let him see the baby either at first.'

'It always surprises me who manages to "have affairs". You'd think most women would have some standards.'

'Thanks. That's exactly the contribution I expected.'

'I'm sorry. I'm only joking. I guess I don't understand why he would do that from his side, and also why some other woman would want to get involved in this mess.'

'This mess being that he's poor and down on luck? But it's OK for rich, fortunate people to sleep around? You really live in a different world, don't you?'

'No, the mess being that he's married, has a child, and ... fine, he isn't the greatest catch overall. But thankfully I do live in a different world, yes. Don't look so shocked. So do you. I don't care if you grew up with these people, and you have undesirable biological links to them. You know that you have nothing in common.'

'That doesn't give you the right to talk about them like this though.'

'You know what? We should talk about something else.'

'We should, yes. Do you want to talk about the fact that Jen was laid off last month and she's now staying here with the baby, as well?

'Oh, that's the baby. This isn't happening. You're just telling me stories you've seen on daytime TV, aren't you?'

'You are lovely today. Why did you come to visit again?'

'I'm sorry, but you're telling me that I have to stay here for a week and share a house with your mom, your dad, your unemployed depressive brother, his estranged resentful wife and their infant?'

'Sorry, we didn't know you were coming. We would have evacuated the house otherwise, because after all the whole world, even in Thoreau, New Mexico, revolves around you.'

I figure that this is about the time when I have to start pretending to be nice, so I tell her that the only reason I'm here is that I love her and I want to be with her, that I'm only joking when I say the things I do about her brother but I will now stop, that the people who are important to her are also important to me, and that I don't really mind who's at the house. I make a quick suggestion for both of us to stay in a hotel for the rest of the week which I'll obviously pay for because, sure, I don't mind these living arrangements and I'm very agreeable and everything, but there's a limit, she turns it down and gets in another inexplicable huff, and I finally go upstairs to brush my teeth.

I plug in and turn on my phone and see several messages from Markus spanning the last hour, so I call him back. It's just after 12pm back in LA, meaning that he's been awake since around 11am if not earlier, which is startling, to say the least.

'What are you doing up so early?' I ask.

'OK, here's my story: what time do I usually get up?'

'Um, in the afternoon at some point?'

'Correct. As you know perfectly well, I've got into this very disruptive habit of going to bed very late, and getting up equally late the next day.'

'That's right. Which makes it impossible to get through the incredible bulk of tasks you've set for yourself each day.'

'Exactly. I could be doing so much more with my life, I'm sure.'

'Well, anything's more than nothing, so I'm going to have to agree.'

'Right, well, today is the first day of the rest of my life.'

'A situation completely unique to you, of course.'

Ignoring me, he continues: 'I've decided to start operating on a different time zone, which will progressively alter my body clock making it easier to function on a more conventional time schedule.'

'You have moved all your clocks forward, haven't you?'

'Yes. I'm now on Central, which means that I went to bed last night at 5am, like I usually do, but it was actually 3am here in LA. And I got up at 1pm, but it was actually 11am.'

'You realize you're just playing mind games with yourself, right?'

'Yes, but that means I'll always win. Anyway, it worked last night. I feel like a brand new person. So accomplished. I'll keep Central for a few days, and then I'll move a couple of time zones ahead. I expect that within two weeks, when I'm operating on London time, I'll have caught up with the rest of California.'

'I wish there were an easier way for you to do this, but there clearly isn't.'

'No, there isn't. Anyway. What's going on over there? Has she forgiven you? Have you slaughtered any cattle yet?'

'I think she has, yes. We have other things to argue about already. I was prepared for a week trying to avoid being derisive and snobbish to a pair of ageing country folk, but I didn't know I'd also be rooming with two other generations of the Dalton clan. Her brother's moved back in with his wife and child. And none of these people have any jobs. Come to think of it, her brother is just like you, only without your socially responsible and extremely admirable time zone transition plan.'

He laughs. 'Be careful, Parke. Let me tell you about the very poor. They are different from you and me. They're born with nothing to lose and develop a spiteful grudge against the rest of us early on. Then, they go through life with a feeling that the world owes them, that they've been done wrong. You can't win with people like that; you can't get them on your side.'

'You're possibly right. In any case, I've got to go. I'm supposed to be groveling to Ryan. And I'm starting not to feel well.'

'OK. This doesn't surprise me – you can catch all sorts of nasty things in the country. Talk to you later.'

5

The good thing is that I never get to see Ryan's dad, as he seems to be working these inhumane hours. He gets up around 4.30am and goes to bed very early in the evening, possibly even late in the afternoon, meaning that our paths hardly ever cross. The bad thing is that everyone else seems to always be around. Ben has taken a ferocious dislike to me, which I can't pretend that I'm not enjoying. Our first proper conversation was the most amusing. He asked me what I do for work, not that he has a chip on his shoulder about it or anything, and when I said I'm in computer game development he sneered and went into a rant about all the manual labor he's had to do in his life. He said that at the ripe age of 10 he learned how to butcher a cow and a pig. I didn't ask if this was simultaneously. That he grew up going hunting. That he's worked hard labor in a ranch for almost fifteen years. Well, I thought, fifteen years on and off, mostly off. That he knows what a hard day's work is and how to get his hands dirty without acting like a girl. That he learnt how to drive an 18-wheeler, dump truck, hi-lo and front-end loader. Whatever those are. And that his best ranch memory was mudding (I wasn't aware that 'mud' could be used as a verb and I'm still not aware of what it describes) then mud-wrestling with friends in the middle of a cornfield. Which sounds like something directly out of a gay redneck fetish website, but what do I know?

I think Ben and I are reliving a class war that's as old as time, even though I'm personally in no mood to drag it into the year 2012 and this small town to fight my corner. This quite probably infuriates him more, as it feeds his perception that I'm impassive and comfortable, that I've never had to really work for anything, even if it is to defend myself against his petty, two-bit digs. I want to scream 'I WENT TO HARVARD, YOU BASTARD', but I'm not sure he'll recognize that as a thing. The biggest joke about all this, of course, is that these accusations are coming from a guy who's only awake for around six hours a day and those are mostly spent to bring other people down with a single-minded fixation. I don't understand how somebody with those credentials can place himself on a pedestal of productivity, but I can't really enter the mind of a moneyless apathetic sociopath. Moneyed apathetic sociopaths – fine. Markus has been my case study for that demographic throughout my life.

Ben's wife, Jen, spends most of her time shut in the bedroom that she shares with her baby (a mismatched extension to the rest of the house, which looks like it was built by somebody with Ben's skill and dedication, and probably was) and only ventures out to help cook. I expect she's clinically depressed. As you would be, really, if you woke up one day and realized you're married to Ben, bringing up his child, have lost your job and living in your in-laws' back room. She's also been to a couple of job interviews in the few days that I've spent here, apparently with no luck yet. Going by the few moments that I've been in her company I have no reason not to like her and I actually hope she hasn't fallen too far down this pit of bad luck and bad choices to ever come back.

The child, whose name I'm sure I've been told but I keep forgetting as everyone refers to him as 'Bubba', is mainly looked after by Ryan's mom, followed by Jen, when she's not lost in her dark spells of lifeless self-absorption. I'd be really hard-pushed to recall a single moment when I've seen Ben interact with 'Bubba', so I've grown very suspicious of Ryan's early statement that Jen didn't let him see the baby for a while, as a form of punishment after his affair. It just doesn't seem like something that would cause the least bit of concern to him.

On Friday, our last full day in Thoreau, all these individually alluring members of the Dalton family and I come together to attend the wedding of cousin Denny to – possibly – second cousin, Emmie. It's a joyful occasion by anyone's standards, which introduces me to a plethora of Dalton relatives, both close and distant, and confirms to me that if things are ever to get serious with Ryan and I were to legally bind myself to this extended family, a pre-nuptial agreement should not be merely an optional request.

Still, a day of watching two blood relatives join their lives together in holy matrimony doesn't even come close to the emotional peaks that one experiences from sharing a table with a drunk Ben. In the six, seven, possibly fifty-two hours that we're at this venue he gets progressively blitzed and decides to adopt me as his unlikely best pal. The turning point between being his mortal enemy and beloved confidant is a simple statement of: 'You're alright, you know. Plus you're fucking loaded'. Following that, I get numerous revelations, and by revelations I mean disturbing, probably made-up stories, such as the time when he fucked the girl he was seeing behind his wife's back in the bathroom at her work Christmas party, and the illegal immigration business he's allegedly involved in.

Directly influenced by that, but also from my cumulative experiences in Thoreau over the last few days, I take Ryan for a walk outside and casually tell her that I'm all for being with her, but we have to make a deal and that deal is that I will never, ever, ever have to come to visit her family again, or even enter the state of New Mexico for that matter. This doesn't go down as well as one might have expected and Ryan snaps back at me, saying that I'm pompous, inconsiderate and downright mean and perhaps she doesn't actually want to be with me after all, if this is how I feel about the place where she's from and her family lives, whom she loves more than life itself (this is news to me). I explain that this is no reflection on her, but let's be fucking honest, this is white trash all over and I'm under no obligation to deal with that just because I happen to be her boyfriend. She fails to see my point and retorts that having a white trash family is better than having a family that doesn't love me and has never had an interest in me. I'm not sure I like what I'm hearing, so I ask her to elaborate so that she can dig herself further into that particular hole, something that she seems more than happy to do by telling me that it's quite clear really: my father is a drug addict that didn't even know of my existence until I was a few years old and my mother is simply one of those people that were never meant to have children, because she's quite extraordinarily fucked up.

Following those statements, I storm out, drive back to that shocking barn she calls home, pick up my stuff and head to Albuquerque to spend the night in a hotel, intending to catch the first morning flight back to LAX. Well, first morning flight after I've naturally woken up. Getting to Albuquerque is excruciating – being in a state of blind rage isn't conducive to a gentle drive, it seems – and before I fall asleep, I feel the need to get in and out of bed, turn the TV on and off, brush my teeth and flush the toilet four times each to calm myself down.

Just after 10 o'clock in the morning, I'm woken up by a persistently ringing cellphone. Why it's not on silent, I'll never know. Answering semi-conscious I'm faced with an agitated Ryan asking what I'm doing and why I haven't picked up her last five calls. I tell her that I'm sleeping, of course, and also I didn't know that we were now on speaking terms. She says that perhaps we should both just grow up, and anyway something's happened and she wants to talk to me. I tell her that I'm still not happy about the things she said about my family last night, and if she wants me to stay on this call, she had better apologize. She says that it was really inappropriate of her to say those things and kinda drifts off, and even though this doesn't lead up to the apology I had envisaged, I decide to pretend to be nice (plus I want to hear what god damn terrible thing has happened, keeping my fingers crossed that it involves Ben) and ask her what's up.

As it turns out the story does involve Ben, though unfortunately not in the role of the victim. When the Daltons went home last night after the wedding, he stayed up drinking alone and thought that it would be a good idea to supplement with some sedatives, which he has a prescription for and regularly uses because, you know, he's so depressed and everything. He was discovered passed out, but still breathing, on the kitchen table after 5am when the other members of the family freakishly got up to have breakfast despite it being the weekend and was more or less carried to the back room to continue his stupor. Two or three hours later Bubba was observed crawling sluggishly around the house, knocking into chairs, doorframes, and the odd house pet.

Panicked by a drowsiness that they couldn't shake out of him, Jen and grandparents desperately tried to diagnose the semi-conscious infant until they made the discovery of a half-chewed Valium tablet on the laminate kitchen floor, just behind one of the table legs. When Bubba made a feeble but unambiguous attempt to grab it and stick it in his mouth, the penny dropped. He was buzzed off his tiny head. Fueled by anger and worry, Ryan's dad decided to make a spasmodic attempt to regain control over the frazzled family he's supposed to be heading (a clear case of too little, too late) and stormed into Ben's room for a confrontation, as Jen and Ryan's mum rushed to the hospital. Ryan doesn't know what form the confrontation took – there was a lot of shouting – but her dad eventually emerged from the room with the information that Bubba can't have swallowed more than one and a half tablets of Valium, as Ben only had two left after taking his dose (and they found half in the kitchen). Still, 7.5mg of Diazepam isn't desirable for a toddler, or so I hear.

At the time that Ryan is telling me all this, the child is out of danger and on his way back, her dad has gone to be next to some animal somewhere and her brother is back asleep. Nothing ever changes.

'The more time I spend here … the less time I want to spend here,' she says.

'Come on then. Come with me now.'

'My flight's tomorrow. What's the point in leaving one day early?'

'You just said that you hate it here. I think you've stayed long enough. It's up to you though, I don't care either way.'

'Wait. Do you think I can change the flight?'

I sigh. 'What does it matter? I haven't even booked a flight for myself. Come to the airport with me and I'll buy us both tickets.'

'I think I will. Thank you.'

'No problem. It's because you're so nice to me.'

'Aha.'

'Sorry, I'm joking. Come on over then. I'll meet you at the airport in two hours. We'll get the first flight out of here after that.'

6

Back in LA later on Saturday evening we spend the night pretending that we're happy in this relationship and that we haven't just wasted the last week tearing each other apart. Well, there's still a small argument that takes place between us and it revolves around what we'd rather do – Ryan wants us to stay in and watch a movie and wash each other's hair or whatever it is that she imagines content, grown up couples do, and I want to go to this party we've been invited to at the Beverly Hilton, just for a couple of hours, where some people might even be that I actually like. We end up staying in. She insists that we watch some Technicolor movie from the 1950s called *Rear Window* and I have to question how old this woman actually is, but to be fair once I give up my preconceptions I get sucked in and find it very enjoyable. Particularly after I kick Markus out, who's ruining the mood by being stoned and contributing nothing but derisive, moronic comments. The evening peaks around midnight when I come inside Ryan's mouth, whilst thinking of the blonde actress from the movie, Grace Kelly, I think, trying to block out the fact that this actress looks a bit like my mom when she was younger. Actually, a lot like my mom when she was younger.

On Sunday morning Ryan wakes up at some unfeasibly early hour again, presumably still influenced by her 5.30am rises over the past week, but there are no chickens to feed or bread dough to knead in my apartment, so when I get up just before 11am, I find her sitting outside by the pool, reading. Markus is also there doing laps, which means that his time zone transition plan must really be working. The three of us decide to go out for breakfast or early lunch or whatever this is and head back inside to get ready. Looking into my closet I see one t-shirt out of place, pulled out slightly to stick out from the rest of the pile, so I ask Ryan whether she's been going through my stuff while I've been asleep. She takes this as her cue to give me a look that's explicitly querying whether I've lost my mind, but we narrowly escape another argument as it suddenly clicks to me that I deliberately pulled this shirt out of place myself last night, so that I remember to wear it in the morning. I ask Ryan whether she's impressed that my younger self by ten hours outsmarted my current self temporarily, she tells me that 'impressed' is not the word she's thinking right now, we go pick up Markus and leave.

We're at this place called Bread on 3rd Street – the three of us, plus a friend of Ryan's from work that she's invited along. I don't really know why Ryan has chosen to be friendly to this girl, Reed. I've met her several times and she's pleasant enough, but really so plain both in terms of looks and personality. I mean she's not dumb, but she's definitely not one to go for the limelight. Perhaps this is the appeal. She's the anti-LA girl and I frequently think that Ryan can't stand most of the other girls that we know in this city; one might argue, with good reason.

Reed has never met Markus before. Her perception of him, I'm sure, is the usual one he always leaves on girls of that particular type: an initial, automatic infatuation caused by his almost mechanical, faultless appearance, followed by a subtle aversion knowing that he will almost certainly overlook her, followed by quiet contentment with the situation, seeing that he's so unstable that you wouldn't want to spend much time in his company no matter what he looks like. This final stage usually occurs once the 'plain girl' type has had a brief conversation with him. There are many other girls, of course, who retain a very keen interest even after they've come to know him inside out, but those girls are usually so self-involved and caught up in their own drama and importance that Markus' personality failings pale in comparison.

During this lunchtime, Reed's moves down the trajectory from inadvertent infatuation to conscious rejection very swiftly, as a consequence of a story he decides to tell about his forearm tattoo. The thing is, Markus has got this dark block of ink there, spanning the inside of his left arm from the wrist to just below the inside of his elbow. It's just a stark, black rectangular and it looks like it's covering something, a regretful earlier tattoo, simply because it doesn't make sense that this design would be someone's first choice. I don't know how he dreamt this one up, or whether this was always the intention, to play this game, but he now takes great pleasure in telling people different stories about what it hides when they ask.

When Reed makes the mistake of enquiring, he goes into this ridiculously elaborate story, which goes as follows:

He got the first, regretful tattoo when he was 18, apparently. During the summer after graduating from high school he started seeing this girl, Carrie, who went to the same school as we did, only a few years below. She was just 14. Most people knew Carrie, despite her being a freshman, and most people felt equally sorry for and intimidated by her. This was the outcome of the unique circumstance for our school, a school where most parents where interlinked somehow, of having lost her mother when she was very young, maybe even at childbirth – this was obviously a sensitive point that no one would dare probe, not the way anyone in our school was raised – and being brought up in disgusting wealth by a father involved in very, very dubious activities. Was he controlling drug trafficking operations on a very high level across the Bay Area? Was he involved in arms smuggling across North Africa? Was he a porn baron capitalizing on the extensive talent all across the coast from San Diego to San Francisco? Well, OK, up to Santa Cruz perhaps. There's no talent in San Francisco. Something unwholesome like that anyway. What brought Markus and Carrie together was an unhealthy obsession with weed. What kept them going was the long, lazy summer. Neither of them had anything to do, so they just wasted time getting stoned around the city, completely consumed in their teenage love.

Over one of those endless warm nights during the end of August when they would both stay up getting more and more out of it, Markus and Carrie decided that it would be a pretty decent idea to get a pair of DIY tattoos. He was constantly stoned and drunk at that point. Carrie scrawled her name on his forearm with a biro in very elaborate, big-looped handwriting and then took to tracing it with a needle she was dipping in ink. He wrote his last name more modestly in small capital letters on the inside of her right thigh and did the same. Needless to say, the whole affair didn't last very long after that. Something about both of them getting progressively more lethargic and spiritless because of the drugs, something about Carrie's father finding out about the affair and making a few life threats, nothing major though, and Markus had broken it off by early September. He had to wait a month or so for the DIY mess on his arm to heal and as soon as that happened her went and had it covered with this block straightaway.

Admittedly, this is one of Markus' most intricate tattoo cover-up stories, one that leaves me almost impressed even although I've already heard too many of them. Reed seems aghast and quite incredulous, but she's too timid to challenge him directly and Ryan just looks annoyed, thinking that he's mocking her friend. This, of course, is not really the case and Markus would have told this story to anyone, no matter how insipid they were.

After lunch Ryan and I go for a drive up on the Hills where we stop and take pictures of each other pretending to snort the Hollywood sign in the distance behind us, but it's soon late afternoon and she wants to go back home. Ryan seems to have a problem with Sunday afternoons, meaning that she starts stressing out about the impending working week and doesn't want to do anything but sit indoors and wait for Monday morning as the crippling gloom envelopes her. I sort of think that if she dislikes her job so much, if that is her problem, perhaps she should find a different one.

Personally, I'm very happy to go into work, keep myself busy for a while and talk to the people there. The difference might be that I don't actually have to. I work as a freelancer for a gaming company that makes iPad and console games. I started doing something similar in my last year in college, working for a couple of tiny companies based east at first before moving back to California and getting this job with one of the medium-sized firms based here in LA in Burbank. Doing this is good for my personality, I'm sure, because otherwise, I guess I would be, well, Markus really. As I don't necessarily have to go into the office to do the work (even though I often prefer to) it's not a permanent position, and I don't need the money it pays me – which goes directly to one of the charities my family's trust supports – I never feel tied down, obliged to be there.

What I also don't feel obliged to do is waste my evening sitting there with Ryan waiting for the night to fall. Back home, I walk over to Markus', turn his music down and ask him for ideas of people to contact. He says that Party Boy Michael Murphy always has a buzz around him, particularly on Sundays, so we give him a call and he says that sure, he's going to some drinks type thing at this house in Laurel Canyon. Sven and Bjorn's house, apparently. Do we know them, Michael asks. We confirm that we don't.

Even so, we can tag along anyway, Michael is sure of it. I like Michael. He's very well connected, severely hedonistic and always up to something. You don't get a nickname like that for nothing. I tell Ryan that I'm heading out for a bit and ask her if she wants to come with (she doesn't).

'OK, I promise that I won't be late.'

'Oh, why don't I believe that?' she asks.

'Wanna bet $50?'

'I don't want to take your money, you pitiful individual,' she says with affectionate scorn, if there is such a thing, and I leave.

Markus and I drive together and pick up Michael. The party where he takes us is moderately sized: maybe thirty, forty people come and go during the time that I'm there. Despite Michael's reputation the buzz is only moderate at best and Markus is soon the most wasted person in attendance – the result of a couple of Es and the unidentified leftover contents of two small plastic bags he brought with him and not sharing with anyone on top of whatever coke is doing the rounds. I don't know how long exactly we've stayed, but I know that it's time to go when he comes back after having disappeared for a while and says that he's just been upstairs and seen what he thought was a painting, until he walked through it. After I drive us back home and go to my apartment, Ryan's in bed and not acknowledging my return, which I suspect is a sign that she's mad at me, but it wasn't my fault. I would have left earlier, had Markus and I driven in separate cars.

7

On Monday morning Ryan gets up at 7am and makes a point of waking me up at the same time by opening the curtains and being exceptionally noisy. She starts work at 8.30am and I don't go into the office until around 10am, but this is not very important; what's happening here is that she's getting her own back for me coming home late. Transparent and resentful as this is, I decide it might be a good idea to play along and I get up without complaining. I do want to be in this relationship after all…don't I?

She's not ready to let go.

'Aren't you tired?' she says when I walk in the kitchen.

'No, I'm fine.' I really am fucking not.

'Can't imagine you got as much sleep as you usually need.'

'I got enough, thanks.'

'You could always go back to bed. It's not like you have to be anywhere for another two hours. If at all.'

'You try sleeping with all the light and noise around.'

'Oh, I'm sorry. I had to get up. Some of us actually have to work.'

'I'm going to work too.'

'Right, right. Otherwise you might not be able to pay your rent.'

'That's rich. You practically live here. I don't see you paying for anything.' She literally gasps. This is going very well, I reckon.

'You know, it's fine that you've always had it all on a plate. But to make a fucking pretense that you actually have to try for anything…'

'Ooh, expletives. Did they teach you to talk like this at BU? Or was it Thoreau's fine high schools?'

She fixes her eyes on mine, says 'worthless' with what she perceives to be time-stopping intensity and makes for the door.

'Why am I doing this?' I'm thinking. 'Why don't I end it?' No, it's fine. There are some positives: The parts of her brain that don't begrudge me. The most obscenely high cheekbones I've ever seen. The fullest lips. Her thin, long limbs. The bored look she wears when she's distracted, like it's a huge drag for her to even exist. How everyone thinks we're a great couple. The fact that she cares enough to try to make me a better person. This relationship is good for me, it's good for me, it's good for me. I sip the rest of my coffee reading the news on my laptop, get ready and drive to work early.

My office is in an excruciatingly modern complex in Burbank, north of Los Angeles. All glass buildings, artificial lakes, and steel bars holding up extraneous outdoor canopies. A 21st century landscape architect's unimaginative modernist vision, actually very similar to my apartment block in Westwood. I've always thought that there's nothing wrong with a bit of traditional architecture, though I suppose I'm not in the right place for it. Not to mention that not many computer games design firms are based in brownstone 19th century buildings.

The floor that I work on is not a bad one when it comes to the social opportunities. It's an open plan office, like everything is, and I'm sitting with a mix of tech geeks and business/administration people. The tech geeks spend the day drawing sketches for games, putting together design documents, writing code and pseudocode, refreshing DailyTech and Wired, sending cat memes around to each other, and looking down on the business people for being too dumb and having only basic skills, the type that you readily pick up in business school. Conversely, the business people spend their days making phonecalls, organizing meetings, talking to clients, refreshing Buzzfeed and Mashable, sending cat memes around to each other (cat memes are universal and transcend all office cliques) and looking down on the tech geeks for being too awkward, weird and, well, geeky.

Then, of course, there are also the girls from Human Resources, who utilize their very limited roster of skills to circulate memos, print out employment contracts, organize staff events, and spread work gossip. They are also available for office-based affairs, or the fantasy of pursuing one with them anyway. I'm pretty sure that most of them understand the empowerment that being sexually desirable provides and they want to enhance their prominence in the workplace, so they feed people's interest by wearing borderline acceptable outfits for an office environment and subtly, but definitely noticeably, flirting with everyone.

From where my desk is, I have a quite decent view of people from all these departments. In fact, we don't all sit separately. Apart from the HR girls who occupy a hub to the side of the rectangular open-plan office about halfway through, everyone else is mixed in. This is the advantage of having an integrated, unrestricted office culture, which extends to the seating arrangements. The disadvantage of having an integrated, unrestricted office culture is that I'm also sitting near the much-loathed, despicable company Managing Director. In fact, I'm not just sitting near him. I'm sitting at the same cluster of four desks as him, with his seat being diagonally opposite mine facing me, making him the person I see clearest, closest and most directly when I'm sat at my desk.

Oh how we loathe this guy. Theo Rothchild. No, not Rothschild, like the banking family, but Rothchild. Missing the 's', but making up for it in sheer pompousness, self-assurance and grandiosity. Never has a glorified middle manager originally from fucking Minnesota carried oneself around with such ceremony before. He was regretfully plunged into Neon Sphere, our company, about three months ago, soon after we were taken over by VisionONE, a large software group based in Cupertino. Apparently they were not happy with the way things were running, even though we were a healthy, profitable little company with a steady growth, so they brought Theo in to fix us. He landed as Managing Director out of nowhere, armed with a million ideas of how everything could be improved: from the minor (dress-code, office decor) to the paradigm shifting (business plan, working hours) and everything in between.

In terms of his popularity, things got worse within the first month of Rothchild being there. By that point everyone had realized that this person was a complete outsider, with little to no knowledge of our industry, a plain hire-a-suit who seemingly was here to roll out his tired and tested cookie-cutter management techniques, completely lacking any understanding of who we are or what we do. Prompted by the wave of discontent that was rising within the company, my colleague Rich Cerna investigated his background only to discover that Rothchild had made a career out of entering companies at a top level and enforcing his ambitious yet unsuccessful practices before moving on to the next failed endeavor twelve to eighteen months later. Circulated in an email that was prefaced by a revelatory bon mot ("Theo is an enigmatic figure who basically embodies what is wrong with this country in general and its corporate culture in particular. He's also a fucking cunt") this was the final nail on Rothchild's Neon Sphere coffin. We all started hating him, although it seemed that, if the past is anything to go by, we would be stuck with him for another year, maybe year and a half.

On this Monday at work I'm alternating between writing a storyboard for a generic shoot 'em up called Disobey IV: Prison Cell and preparing some pictures on Photoshop annotating the player experience for a new computer game that's based on a huge spy franchise – probably one of about three hundred spy-related games available on the market. There is a big cultural niche for that whole international spy/GQ magazine sort of thing though, which means there's a lot of fucking dull people out there who go through their miserable lives fantasizing about money, power and women. Kinda have to feel sorry for the type of person who buys our games.

What else is going on at work today is that we have a new office color scheme. This was another of Rothchild's masterstrokes – when he first arrived, he took a look around, raised a disapproving eyebrow and decided to have the whole office repainted. This would drive us all up into productivity frenzy, apparently, increasing revenue, profit margins, synergies, and whatever else buzzword they taught him in his second-rate college. The paintwork has been taking place over the weekend and today we walked in to a bright orange office with interspersed lime lines here and there. I think he's taken the 'Neon' from Neon Sphere and run with it. Quite frankly, I feel like going back to my car and getting my sunglasses. In addition, the four separate meeting rooms have been painted yellow, purple, red and green and are now to be referred to as 'the lemon room', 'the grape room', 'the cherry room' and 'the broccoli room' respectively. I object to this one two main levels. First of all I will never, ever book a serious work meeting with anyone and put down 'grape' as the location in my calendar, because some suit with a Midwestern accent decided it was cute. Second of all, and this really bugs me, why are three of the assigned names fruits and the fourth is a vegetable? It's as if he couldn't come up with a green fruit in the six seconds of thought that he put into this whole thing.

As if we haven't had enough of Rothchild's tyranny for one morning, at 11.30am Jamie Tank, Head of Finance and one of Rothchild's most conspicuous yes-men, sends the following email around to everyone in the company:

Dear All,

This is in reference to the use of freelancers, contractors and employees on short-term contracts.

Nobody should commit to the use of any of the above without the prior authorization of Theo or myself. If you feel there is a need for the use of a freelancer, contractor or employee on a short-term contract, you will need to provide a satisfactory explanation on why that need can't be serviced by an existing permanent member of staff.

If you have any questions, feel free to let me know.

Best regards,

Jamie Tank

Now, I'm not a very suspicious person, but I can't help but feel that this new commandment might be quite explicitly directed at me. This is perhaps linked to the fact that I'm the only freelancer currently working at Neon Sphere. Rothchild has never been a big fan of mine, and I can't think why, apart from the fact the my eyes are in severe danger of rolling back into my head every time he opens his mouth to make some laughable announcement or attempt motivational business chat. I'm also probably the only person who's refused to take note of this new working hours he introduced, extending our working day by an hour – 9.30am to 6.30pm. I still turn up at 10am and leave around 6pm as my initial agreement specified. But I think what cuts him up the most is that every time he's tried to make a connection with me, bringing up my name and the businesses that my family owns (because he's a desperate social climber) I've refused to engage.

As soon as I've read Jamie's email, I forward it to Rich and comment:

'Well it looks like I won't be working on Disobey V or the sequel to this shitty spy game after all.'

Rich writes back:

'Haha – do you know what, I thought exactly the same thing.'

'I detest this crackdown.'

'Me too. Who would we laugh with if you weren't here?'

'Hopefully they will have got over it within the next month or so.'

'Knowing this place, there will be a whole new management team by then.'

'Exactly. With a whole new office color scheme as well.'

'Oh, I hope not. I love the colors.'

'You are joking? I feel like I'm working in a youth center in a rough urban area somewhere in Manhattan circa 1988, where one day one of the head social workers decided to have all the kids paint the place in basic "happy" colors in a contrived attempt to provide a distraction form the gun crime that surrounds them.'

'This is amusing. Probably because it's true. They did a similar brightly-colored paint job at my old office once, including adding catchphrases from games we were producing all over the walls. And they used blackboard paint in one of the meeting rooms so everyone could be "creative". Anyway, I imagine what Rothchild says at the moment goes, so you're stuck with it.'

8

On Thursday evening of the same week, Ryan and I haven't wanted to murder each other for exactly three and a half days, which is a new relationship record and a good enough reason to celebrate with dinner at Chateau Marmont. We get the right looks while we're there and that's good enough for me, plus Ryan gets yet another free dinner in a place she would normally not have heard of, so everyone's a winner.

I drop her off at her place and go home, where Markus is expecting me with some big, no wait, huge news.

'I've spent quite a significant part of the day considering whether I should get a cat,' he says, making himself comfortable on my sofa with some weird weed smoking device that's supposed to minimize the smoke I keep complaining about.

'No, you shouldn't,' I cut him off. 'You can't even take care of yourself.'

'Sometimes your words are like knives, Parke,' he says. 'No really though; hear me out.

'This thought came to me late on Sunday night, or Monday morning, call it what you like, when I was I bed, half asleep in my empty apartment. At one point, a conversation from this dinner thing I went to on Saturday started playing in my head. It was basically Thiago Fisher talking about ghosts and saying that he's just seen one this past week.'

'Was there any food at this dinner or just weed?'

'There was. Anyway, as soon as he mentioned the ghosts I had to leave the room, because of my phobia.'

'I don't remember that you ever had a phobia of ghosts. You really need to cut down on the drugs.'

'Sure I did. By the way, in case you haven't noticed, I haven't asked for your contribution so far. I'm trying to tell a story and you keep interrupting me.'

'I'm sorry.'

'It's fine.' He inhales from his weird device and goes into a coughing fit. I walk over and open the balcony door to let some air in.

He stops coughing and continues:

'So even hearing that much of the story was enough to keep me awake two days later. And as I was lying in bed, I thought "wouldn't it be pretty neat if I had a cat here to keep me company?" I don't know exactly what the cat would do to protect me from all those ghosts, but it seemed like a comforting idea. Now here's where you come in. See? There was a part for you always. How do you view me as a potential cat owner?'

'Well, cats are all over the internet right now, so you could be huge on Tumblr. Before you go on, I have a question for *you* – unrelated. When was the last time you had sex with anyone?'

'I don't know. A few months ago.'

'Do you think maybe this is clouding you state of mind, your motivations, everything that you get involved in?'

'No. Can you please answer my cat-related questions now?'

'Shoot.'

He gets his phone out and starts reading a list that he's saved in his notes. Seems very organized. Maybe I misjudged him.

'Is a cat difficult to maintain or is it quite self-sufficient?'

'What does it run on?'

'Can I get a white cat with blue eyes?'

'What should I name it?'

'What do you do when you get bored of it?'

'Are these all your questions? I think you're ready, actually,' I say.

'I think so too.'

'Seriously though, I'm going to start drafting a letter to the ASPCA and I'll put it in the mail the moment you purchase this cat. You have the attention span of a senile moth and you'd be bored of it within three weeks. Maximum.'

'Well if that happens, I'll just open my front door, push it outside and leave it there.'

'Outside your front door is my corridor, no thanks.'

He appears lost in thought. Maybe he's reconsidering. Either that or he's enjoying a pretty good buzz right now.

I go to the bathroom and when I come back he resumes.

'Hm. I actually don't think that my idea of shutting the cat outside the front door would be effective in the long term, because every time

I come back home it will be there waiting and trying to sneak in behind me. And this could get tricky when I come back with lots of shopping from Trader Joe's in my hands and have less flexibility of movement.'

'There you go, problem solved – no cat. Plus, do you realize they live for fifteen to twenty years?'

'I see. I have to be honest. This is another knockback to my plan. I really don't have time for any of this.'

'Good. Back in the real world, I'm going to bed.'

On Friday I wake up early, just before 9am, and I'm feeling OK, so I decide to go to the office and possibly do some work, annoy Rothchild with my presence, maybe play with the HR girls a little bit.

When I get there, I go straight to the kitchen to get some bagels, where I find Elina Pankowski from Sales having cornered Rich and keeping him captive with another trademark enthralling story. I'm trying not to listen, just limiting my contribution to giving Rich a compassionate, I-know-what-you're-going-through type of look, but it's very hard to ignore Elina's enthusiastic, exuberant tone and I catch random phrases like 'Paris is always a good idea' and 'if you want to be happy, then be', which Rich deflects by concentrating really hard on the coffee machine that's preparing his espresso, whilst forcing a polite smile.

Of course, I imagine it's very easy for Elina to embrace quotes such as these. From what I understand she grew up in upstate New York, went to a private (likely all girls) school and on to a private (possibly all girls) university. I imagine her father is something like a lawyer, her mother a homemaker, community activist or perhaps teaches a course at a local college (to show she actually has some use for the Master's or PhD in Women in Political America she obtained prior to having Elina). As a girl Elina probably spent her summers at 'away camp' in upstate New York or Connecticut, swimming, canoeing, making yarn bracelets, forming friendships. After high school she spent a summer backpacking in Europe with her two best girlfriends. And after university she moved to Los Angeles and her father's connections helped her land a couple of internships with various associates and eventually this position with Neon Sphere. So, you see, life has always been very easy for Elina and why shouldn't it be?

Because Elina's life has been so wholesome and blessed, she finds it necessary to share every little aspect of it in full detail with anyone who'll listen, as well as those who most certainly won't. Even so, there's something in Elina's tone whilst talking to Rich in the kitchen today that's more manic, more eager, more desperate than usual. As soon as Rich and I are sitting back at our desks, I find out why.

Rich emails me in all caps:

'SHE GOT ENGAGED. As you can imagine, it's only 10.15am and everyone's heard the story twice already.'

I've never met Elina's boyfriend, now fiancé, but I have seen him through some Facebook stalking, and at a first glance he looks like your average Arab American entertainment lawyer who's able to keep himself in expensive suits and sports cars primarily via family money.

I write back:

'Should you tell me this now, or should I wait to hear it straight from the horse's mouth? Wait, what am I asking, tell me now. Then when she corners me, I can just tell her I've heard, congratulate her and run away. Meet me in "broccoli" in thirty seconds.'

In the hideous green meeting room, Rich closes the door behind us and begins:

'OK, I'll just try to give you some edited highlights, because I'm not really up to repeating the full 25-minute story. I will keep it as close to the original delivery as possible though, there are too many highlights for me to spoil with paraphrasing. Here goes. As you probably don't know and don't care, Elina's just come back from a skiing vacation in Aspen. At the end of one of several extremely satisfying skiing days on perfect powder snow...'

'Um, how? It's the end of the season, all that's left there right now is brown slush, I'm sure of it,' I interrupt.

'I don't know. Anyway, listen to me. At the end of one of several extremely satisfying skiing days on perfect powder snow, Amir insisted that they both take the lift up one last time for a final run. Elina was very tired by that point and wanted to go back and sink in a hot tub with a glass of champagne or some organic hot chocolate or whatever, but Amir became very insistent and she decided to indulge him and go up once more, because she loves him so much and shit. When they got to the top, instead of going straight down, Amir lay down on the fresh, unspoilt snow and asked Elina to lay next to him. Elina thought he was being considerate, as she'd just told him she was so tired, etc, and wanted to allow both of them a bit of a rest. Then suddenly, Amir goes down on one knee...'

'I thought they were lying down.'

'Alright, then suddenly, Amir goes up on one knee and proposes.'

'With no ring?'

'With a ring.'

'Weren't they wearing gloves?'

'I swear to God, I'm going to walk away, just listen. If you have any questions, go raise them with Elina.'

'Right, so Amir proposes and – get this – Elina starts giggling for about ten minutes. Then... she asks him to ask again.'

I snort.

'So he asks again on her request, because she ruined the moment with her unstoppable giggling, apparently, she finally says yes and they go down. Back home, she runs in and tells her girlfriend Amanda, who's like a sister to her and happens to be on the same vacation with her perfect boyfriend that she got engaged to two weeks earlier, and – this is the highlight of the story and it's an exact quote from Elina – "Amanda... literally... screams... the chalet... down."'

'Where did they stay after that?'

'I don't know. Again, this is a direct quote for Elina. Anyway, that's all. I have to go back and do some work now.'

'OK, that sounds boring, but let's go.'

Back at my desk, I have two emails from a client about the storyboard I'm working on, one email from my line manager about the same thing, one email from Ryan, and one email from Kurt Morency, a guy from Marketing who's unfortunate enough to be sitting within earshot of Elina.

Ryan has written:

'Good morning, how are you today? Thanks again for dinner last night. What did you do when you got home? I missed waking up next to you this morning.'

I reply:

'Morning, baby. I'm great. Just got lots of work to do. I missed you too. Do we have any plans for tonight? Let's go out. Or stay in together.

Whatever you want.'

I send this and open Kurt's message, which says:

'I'm sure you've heard Pankowski's awesome news!!!!! Probably not as many times as I have though. She's practically repeated the same story to every client and supplier she's answered the phone to. It seems to be the first thing that comes out of her mouth, as soon as she picks up the phone. I think somebody actually had the wrong number, and they still got to hear the story before they hung up. I'm starting to fear for my sanity.'

I write back:

'You're right, I have heard the news. Ohmagawd, I'm so excited!! I was scared for quite a while that Amir would never come through, but look at him now, he proved all of us wrong.

Seriously though, it didn't even cross my mind that this ruthless over-sharing included phone calls. I thought it was just co-workers. This changes things completely. We can now also assume that no one is safe: anyone who sends her an email (even spam), delivery guys, passers-by on the street. What a nightmare. I couldn't care less about 99.8% of the people on this planet, but suddenly I feel almost ill for them.

I have to say, I haven't heard the story first-hand myself. Rich just repeated it for me. I'm going to do my best to avoid her all day, maybe this month actually.'

'I'm in love with the suggestion that she replies to spam emails sharing her news. I want this to be happening.

As for you, just stay clear off the kitchen area. That's where she usually prowls, pouncing on unsuspected, hungry victims as soon as they enter. I can't imagine you want to risk it, even if you were starving.

Charlotte Ryland from Accounts sneaked into the kitchen earlier when she thought Elina wasn't looking, but before she had the chance to take the milk for her cereal out of the refrigerator, she saw her walking over. She grabbed the first things she could get her hands on from around there and fled back to her desk. She's now eating three coffee-stained napkins, a piece of burnt sourdough bread left in the toaster and the remnants from a can of evaporated milk.'

I type, 'Thanks for the heads up. It's like Armageddon; you do what you can to survive' and go back to my storyboard.

Half an hour or so later I get an email from Ryan:

'I'm sure this won't go down very well with you. But Trevor messaged me on Facebook last night. He's in LA just for the weekend and he asked if I wanted to have a drink. He's here for an exhibition, he said. Would you mind if I went to meet him for an hour? I won't go if you don't want me to. I just don't want to be rude.'

I'm now really pissed off. This is the ex that she never really loved. This is the fucked up ex that she only stayed with for so long, because she was afraid what he might do to himself – or possibly her – if she broke up with him. This is the human wreck that, when they finally broke up, completely lost it, broke down doors, threatened to kill himself, went on week-long drinking benders and landed in jail multiple times. Has she forgotten all this? Has she forgotten the incident when he deliberately drove them off the road and into a traffic light weeks after the initial break up, when she was feeling sorry for him and still spending time around him? Or did these things never happen in the first place?

I punch a response in list form:

'a) I thought you had blocked that loser on Facebook

b) He's not here for any exhibition, HE IS NOT AN ARTIST

c) Interesting to know that you're still willing to spend time with your abusive, girlfriend-beating ex; from a psychological point of view, anyway

d) Do what you like. I'll make other plans'

Kinda blinded by fury, I send it off, spot Elina standing in the kitchen area bursting with excitement to share her news, stand up and make my way over.

9

On Wednesday the following week I'm working from home when I get a Facebook group invite from my friend Jeremy Thibeaux, which has gone out to fifteen-twenty people, including Rae Prinz, Tommy Gillman, and Katie, whose last name is Larson it turns out after all. Generally a few of that crowd at the Palm Springs pool party, as well as Markus, Ryan and me. Apparently we're all going to Coachella and we're about to get very, very excited about it.

Now I don't know about Markus, but I certainly don't have a ticket for Coachella myself, so I go next-door to find out. He is, of course, asleep. I scream at him a little and get him out of bed and when he's reached approximately 60% consciousness, I ask:

'What's this about Coachella? Are we going?'

'Not that I know of.'

'Well everyone else seems to be going. We must go.'

'OK. We're going.'

'Where are we supposed to get tickets? It's in two weeks or something.'

'I don't know. Ask around. You've got friends.'

'Fine. Just so you know, if we don't get tickets and we end up not going, I really don't know what I'm going to do. Our lives have been leading up to this for, what is it, twenty minutes now?'

'Pull yourself together, man. You can do it. Meanwhile, I'm going back to bed.'

He goes back in his room, shouts 'get me a ticket too' and closes the door behind him.

Back in my flat, and despite still being kinda mad at her for that meeting with Trevor, I give Ryan a call and tell her that we have to go to Coachella, there's no other option, everyone is going to be there, and what does she want exactly, to isolate us from all of our friends?

She asks me to calm down, asks me who's playing, I say I have no idea, as if she has any idea about music and bands anyway apart from the trite pick-up truck country her parents must have played when she was growing up, she asks me who's going, I keep this very vague, she complains that she can't take any days off work, I say, oh really, I guess you have to keep all your vacation to visit Thoreau, she asks me to stop being obnoxious and says that, fine, she'll go from Friday evening until Sunday.

I hang up, post in the Facebook group asking if anyone has three tickets for sale, someone has three tickets for sale and I buy them.

At this point I sit down to do some work, I swear, but just a few minutes later, Rich emails me from the office:

'Have you seen any good episodes of Columbo recently?'

I write back:

'When you say recently, does 1999 count?'

'Yeah. What's thirteen years ago? It's not even fifteen. So what happened in that one?'

'Someone commits a murder; Columbo swoops in and takes all the glory. Oh, and he was wearing a filthy raincoat. It was a good one.'

'That doesn't sounds familiar, I don't think I've seen that one.'

A few minutes later, I reply:

'Just off the top of my head, I believe the synopsis was something like…

"When Patricia Hunter [Jessica Mulfield], famous daytime television actress, kills Hector Chapman [Cliff Vaughn], her embittered ex-lover, to stop him from publishing a book exposé of her former life as a streetwalker in Chicago, suspicion falls on Hector's stepson, Theodore [Peter Soul], who goes missing right after the murder. But once it turns into a full-blown media event, Theodore resurfaces, explaining he needed some time to himself."

And so on.'

'That's pretty good memory. You've got quite a few details in there, well done. Thanks for linking to the actors' Wikipedia pages too, I've always been intrigued by Jessica Mulfield.

I've got Columbo planned on my TiVo and it records a few episodes a week. I think it's on at 4am or something on some weird mystery channel and there's also a person doing sign language at the bottom of the screen.

It was a little distracting at first, but now I couldn't watch Columbo without it. Also, I'm learning a new language.'

'This is great, Rich. Maybe you can show me something when I'm next in the office. Anyway, why do broadcasters assume deaf people only watch TV at 4am?'

'I think it's a well-known fact that deafness and insomnia go hand-in-hand.'

'Maybe they don't like falling asleep, because they won't hear their alarm?'

'That's probably it. Once they're out, they're out.'

'I know I was joking before, but now I'm actually thinking, has an alarm clock been made for dead people? This is a typo, but I'm leaving it.'

'Calm down, there's probably a vibrating one or something. Maybe one that throws water at them.'

'This isn't a scene from Wallace & Gromit. This is real life, bruh!'

I google Wallace & Gromit, don't get it, eventually write back:

'OK, well, what else is going on over there today?'

'Oh there are some big developments. Rothchild's had a new office chair delivered, just for him. It seems that none of the existing chairs already available on the premises were good enough for him.'

'Why does this guy want people to detest him so much? It's a weird need to have. What's the chair like? I have high hopes for this.'

'Oh it's nothing extraordinary, just your run-of-the-mill high-concept ergonomic kneeling chair with no back.'

'I have no idea what you are talking about.'

He sends me a link. I look it up and write back:

'You mean to tell me that he's sitting there right now on that surrounded by approximately one hundred people sitting on normal chairs that cost one tenth of the price?'

'Yes. He did justify it by saying that he has a bad back and sitting on another chair is simply insufferable. Of course, I'm 100% sure that the high-concept ergonomic kneeling chair has nothing to do with posture and everything to do with posturing.'

'What a cunt. In protest, I will now stop working for the day.'

I check my Facebook to see a message from Katie that says:

'Hiya. Looking forward to partyin at coachella with you!!'

I write back 'You bet. I can't wait – just found ticketd' leaving my typo in so that she doesn't think I care enough to edit my messages for her, send it, delete the conversation and go out to grab some lunch.

When I come back an hour or so later, Markus is in my apartment. He appears quite animated. This is cat-related, I know it.

'Are you ready for this?'

'Probably not.'

'I've found the perfect cat for me. I did an online test asking me all sorts of questions about what I want from my cat and it chose a breed for me. I'm getting a Blue Russian. No wait, it's Russian Blue. Yes, that's cat breed, not a cocktail.'

During this delirium I think all that's required of me is to appear half-interested, perhaps a touch supportive, which seemingly I manage to accomplish, as he continues.

'As you know, Russian Blues are affectionate, playful, and active but not annoyingly so. Also they do this thing where they pick one person in the house where they live as their favorite and they become this person's loyal companion. And because it's only me living at my place, the cat is bound to pick me.'

'What if it picks me?' I interrupt.

'It won't. You've got enough problem getting people to like you, let alone cats.'

'Yes, while you're personable and heartwarming.'

'Thank you. So I've spent the afternoon looking where I can get one online. The bad news is that if I want to get a kitten, which I do, why would I buy someone else's grown-ass cat, I'll have to wait a month or two. Blue Russians...'

'Russian Blues.'

'Ugh, yes, Russian Blues are a very sought after breed, I'm sure you're aware of this, and I have to reserve one before it's even born. Can you help me look? You're better than me at this sort of thing.'

'I'll help you look, you maniac.'

We go online and look around a bit and eventually find an ad for some kittens that he seems to like, born a few weeks ago and available to pick up as soon as possible. The seller is a 'Suzan' from 'California' (unspecified). Of course Markus wants a male kitten, because he wants the exact cat equivalent of himself. I make a point of asking whether we're looking for a kitten with a severe sociopathic disorder in that case, he says no, a balanced one will do, and I write the message for him:

'Hello,

I'm based in LA and I'm very interested in one of your male Russian Blue kittens. Are they still available?

Thanks,

Markus'

Satisfied for the time being, he gives this a rest and we go downstairs for a swim.

10

On Friday I decide to surprise Ryan with a weekend away because I'm very considerate like that, plus her friend Reed just called me and reminded me that it's our one-year anniversary on Sunday, bitterly adding that she knew I would forget. I begrudgingly thank her, book two seats on a flight to San Francisco for early this evening and immediately get in touch with Denning, my mom's household assistant, asking him to book something appropriate for the weekend and send me through the details. From the email that I get an hour or so later, Denning has decided to reserve a modest farmhouse in Monte Rio in the Russian River Valley, yes the whole farmhouse, all eight rooms, which is good enough I think, plus it will make Ryan feel right at home. I message her to tell her I'm picking her up after work, we're stopping by at home to quickly pack, and then we're going away for the weekend, she says 'oh my God, I thought you'd forgotten', I ask her 'how could I' and then I go to work. It's nearly 11am.

The first person that usually greets me when I get to work is Kwasi, the receptionist. Kwasi possibly has a last name, but it's more conceptual, only to be written and never to be said, primarily because nobody knows how to pronounce this particular juxtaposition of consonants anyway. Kwasi is an intriguing character, a mystery of sorts. He speaks in his own dialect of English, comprising simple words in their primary forms, never conjugating verbs or declining nouns. So, for example, 'have you seen the red folders anywhere in the office?' is reduced to a fancy-free 'you see red folder in office?' I find this vernacular delightful, a breath of fresh air, and quite a time-saver if I'm honest.

Kwasi is extremely affable and will always chat to everyone who crosses his path. Saying that, he limits himself to two topics of conversation only: the pleasures of food and the pains of the daily grind. Those are directly related, in fact, as food – mainly deep-fried – is the one thing that gives him the strength to get through each working day. Other than that, work is just a huge drag. Kwasi takes his food very seriously and the only time that I've actually seen him properly upset was a few weeks ago when

Hillary Mendonca from HR cleared the refrigerator, disposing of all the forgotten stale food that people had left in, accidentally also getting rid of the barbecue-sauce chicken drumstick platter he has as post-lunchtime snack. That was not a pleasant afternoon. Discounting this incident though, his manner is always sociable and good-natured. Even when he moans about having to be at work, on a daily basis, he will do it in an affable, humorous way. When you ask him how he is and he replies 'still alive', he says it with a smile. When he speed-shuffles to the exit at the end of each day announcing that he wants to 'get the hell out of here', it's always tongue-in-cheek. Don't get me wrong, he does want to get the hell out of here, but, you know, he's nice about it.

Kwasi is also one of the few people on this planet who treat me with the respect I deserve, always greeting me with 'hello Mr Parke'. Well, 'hello Mistah Pakk' to be precise. He does that to most men, combining the honorific 'mister' with their first name, although I can't say that he saves the same type of esteem for the females in the office. They just have to put up with a derogatory pet name instead.

This morning when I walk in, his greeting is consistent, although he does also add 'How you doin' today, sir?' I tell him that I'm great, ask him how he is, he tells me that he's still alive and that 'it's Friday, you know?' I nod to Charlotte from Accounts who's standing in reception witnessing all this and smirking, and I walk to my desk.

Kwasi does have a point about Fridays, they're not a bad day to be still alive and in the office, and one particular reason for this is that Rothchild is never in. I don't know what sort of deal he's made, where he comes in whenever he pleases, but perhaps I'm not really one to talk. Anyway, whatever his arrangement, everyone at work seems happier when he's not there.

I sit at my desk, turn on my computer, and the first thing I do is send an email to Charlotte:

'Kwasi makes me feel like a plantation owner.'

She writes back:

'HAHA. He makes me feel like a slut by calling me "baby" / "trouble" / "trouble baby". Different ends of the exploitation scale.'

'It's very interesting sociologically. Why does he feel the need to elevate me (as a white male) but diminish you (as a white female)? I feel like I need to explore his motivations.'

'Just talk to him about it like you're friends. Maybe open with the line "aren't women sexy but stupid?"'

'Thank you, that's a perfect conversation starter. I'd have to be direct anyway. I'm not sure that circling around the topic, dropping hints or being subtle would really translate.'

'Exactly. Also, might be worth holding a chicken drumstick in your hand as bait.'

Then I do some work for a bit, and by work I mean look up Monte Rio online and make plans for my weekend with Ryan, and then I receive an email from Elina Pankowski telling everyone in the office that she's baked some cookies 'to celebrate her engagement' and we can all help ourselves to them if we like. Then before I even get the chance to go in the kitchen to check them out I get an email from Kurt who tells me not to bother, because he already has one on his desk and 'it's so buttery that it greased a hole through his timesheet and now he has to print it out again' and then I go out to get lunch.

I'm driving around thinking of where to go when I get a call from Markus sounding quite animated, and there's no question about it, he's got a kitten update. He tells me that the Russian Blue kitten people have written back and it's sounding quite positive, but there's also something odd about it, the email doesn't quite make sense; whatever it is, he can't put his finger on it. I tell him to forward me the email and I'll have a read (because he's also slightly dyslexic). The message reads:

'hello, thanks for contacting me.
i know you will love them. i simply call them lily, they love their name,they are
11 weeks old when ever i call them lily they will run up
to me like a three year old kid,they have a very
beautiful head, ears and coat. they have been raised in
the home with lots of love and care, and are well
socialized with a wonderful temperament they are vet
checked and up to date on all their shots and will need
them only after six months,they are very fine among
kids and other pets like dogs,.birds etc, they will

make a very fine house pet.their face is just too
adorable.they love to run and play.likes
to stop and smell flowers.there are a pleasure to have
around,they are very friendly,playful and has a very good
behavior.very fine where ever i keep them.
they will come along with all her papers,toys and a 1 year health
guarantee. they will bring so much love and joy to your
home or family for the new year.get back to me if you
are interested in them .
regards'

I call him back:

'You realize that there's no cat to be had from these people, don't you?'

'Well, it's a bit strange.'

'Markus. This message looks like it was written by a twitter spambot. It's most likely some sort of scam. Although, I doubt they've even thought it through, because it's highly unlikely they'll get any money before you see the cat. I mean, I really don't know what their plan is, actually.'

'That's why I think it might be legitimate.'

'Trust me. Legitimate is not the word that applies here.'

'I think I'll message them back anyway. It's the only cat I've found that's available now.'

'OK, do what you like, but I've told you what I think.'

'Yeah, thanks. Will you write back to them anyway?'

I sigh and I say that I do. I log on to his email on my phone and type this back:

'Hello,

Thanks for the information. Do you have a male kitten?
How can I arrange the payment? When would I be able to pick up the kitten and where are you based? I live in LA.

Thanks,
Markus'

The afternoon at work is really dragging, which reminds me why I rarely choose to come in. The only incidents that provide moderate comic relief and a way to pass the time are email conversations with Charlotte and Kurt, which I can have from home as well, to be honest. The latest with Charlotte is that Kwasi called her 'his one and only trouble' before slapping her with a knife on the left shoulder as he walked past her in the kitchen. We have no reason to doubt that by the end of next week he'll be calling her 'his ho-bag' and slapping her directly on the ass, with no props, hand-on-cheek. The latest with Kurt is that he's still having affairs with at least a dozen of the girls who are working in the office; affairs, which primarily, well, in fact exclusively, exist in his imagination and his emails to me.

This afternoon, he writes:

'I've come up with a new coding system for sexual practices in the four meeting rooms. As you're well aware this is really needed, because at the moment people just walk in anywhere and do whatever the hell they want. It's confusing. So ongoing, the following rules will apply:

Broccoli Room – Solo activities

Grape Room – Regular fornication

Lemon Room – Kinky stuff

Cherry Room – Gay

I'm going to print out a memo and pass it around before the end of the day.'

'Thanks, it's been absolutely necessary for someone to take responsibility and sort this mess out. I foresee this will project be your legacy at Neon Sphere.

What else can you tell me today? I can't wait for the day to finish.'

'Let's see. Right before lunch Tina from HR gave me a heart-stopping look. And just now, less than ten minutes ago, I was outside the bathroom near the entrance making a call and Hillary went in brushing against me in what I think was a "follow me" way, and not just because I was blocking the door. Seriously haven't got time for all these bitches.'

'Nice. Did you and Hillary do anything sexual then?'

'No, not sexual, no. Fisting isn't "sexual", is it?'

'Not if it's done with love.'

I leave Kurt to pursue his imaginary affairs and check Markus' email.

There's a response about the cat:

'hello
thanks very much for getting back to me. the kittens are 120 dollars each and 40 dollars for transportation. please if that is ok do send me your complete details so that i can send the kitten over to you. Regards suzan'

I call Markus up:
'Have you seen the email she sent? She sounds crazy, I am uber suspicious. She's not answering any questions and she wants to post the cat to you. Can we give up now?'

'No. I want to see where this goes. It might still be real. Who would do all this to get $160 anyway? If it were a scam, wouldn't they be asking for more money?'

'Well she doesn't sound very smart, so perhaps selling fake kittens online for $160 is the greatest heist she could come up with. Fine, I'm going to call her. We don't have a number, do we?'

'No.'

'Very reassuring. OK, I'll email and ask for one.'

I write to Suzan next:

'Thank you.

I'm going to have to ask again:

a) Do you have a MALE kitten to send?
b) How will I make the payment to you?
c) Where are you based?

Could you please give me a phone number where I can call you?

Thanks,

Markus'

Suzan is online, as she promptly writes back:

'hello

  i have a mail kitten and that is what i want to send to you. all you need to do is to send me all your details. we just relocated to san diego a few days ago. we are actually selling them because pets are not accepted in our new home so we urgently need a home for them. we are giving them out with regrets because of their lovely nature but there is absolutely nothing we can do at this point in time. we promise you never have regrets having them. we can arrange for them to be brought to you any day of your choice. all you need to do is to provide the following in formations

full names as on your identity card

full house address

postal code

street

city. we will also want to let you know that if we send the kittens over to you and you do not like them we will be very happy to receive them back.

i am so sorry my little boy immersed my phone in water. i am still to get a new one. please if you can contact me via emails then it will be fine. waiting for your soonest reply.'

I text Markus:

'Check your email. She REALLY wants to mail you a mail kitten. These are genderless kittens that only travel by post. Needless to say, I'm giving up now. You don't know what seven kinds of inbred crazy this 'mail cat' will be. That, or she'll send you a box full of kitten pictures and pretend that's what you were ordering from the beginning. I'll help you look for another cat.'

Markus texts back with a sad face, I wrap up work and drive over to Ryan's office to pick her up.

11

The fact that we have to stay at my old house overnight makes me a little uncomfortable, but we didn't really have a choice after getting to San Francisco so late. The drive up to Monte Rio takes a couple of hours and it's already almost 11pm when we land. Spending time around my mother is a very unpredictable, potentially unsettling experience, which I try to spare most friends and acquaintances, unless they have a very high tolerance of social misconduct or very little connection to their surroundings like, say, Markus. Ryan has met her once or twice before and has been lucky enough to see mostly her good side. This evening she's pretty far-gone, and in the five minutes that I allow us to be in her company, we are treated to some slurred ramblings, followed by an extended kiss on my lips right before we say goodnight, which I really wish Ryan hadn't seen. On Saturday morning I wake up as early as I'm able to – just after 10am – grab Ryan, who's already up, has had breakfast and pacing the garden outside, and get her the hell out of there.

There's something about being on our own together, away from friends, fucked up families and acquaintances that makes us get on better than any other time. I'm not sure what it is. Perhaps I'm not trying to impress, perhaps I'm not distracted by the shiniest new person that's around, perhaps Ryan feels more relaxed and confident in the knowledge that for this time I'm hers and hers alone (some people need that). One might think that this is a promising sign for our relationship – the fact that we actually seem to like each other. One might also think though that this isn't a realistic way to be. Do we need to completely isolate ourselves from the rest of the human race to appreciate each other? Is a post-apocalyptic planet following a nuclear catastrophe the only habitat where our love can survive?

Waiting for the apocalypse, Monte Rio is the best we're going to get for the time being and the weekend definitely falls under the 'enjoyable' category. Scenic drives, quaint farmhouses, redwood forests, windy roads, riverside fucking, it's all very good, although if

I'm honest, by Sunday afternoon I'm ready to leave this all behind, turn my phone back on (Ryan has imposed a 24-hour ban on cellphone communication with the outside world, cruelly *including* data) and rejoin my absolute favorite: western, shallow civilization. Then of course we get back home on Sunday evening and Ryan tells me she's known all along that I'd forgotten about our anniversary and that I only planned all this last minute, which I suspect is intended to make me feel bad about myself (especially as it's accompanied by her presents to me, a painstakingly put-together photo album of our past year together and a pair of Wayfarers she can barely afford on her Boston University-graduate salary) but in fact it only makes me mad at that sneaky bitch Reed, who grassed me up. Regardless, I take the high road and attempt to be cordial, so I admit to it, apologize profusely, add that I don't deserve her and ask her in what I intend to be a cute, self-effacing way 'why she loves me so much'. She replies that, if I must know, most of the time her love for me is an internal turmoil between 'why the fuck' and 'oh all right then', and I leave it there.

I don't go into the office until Wednesday, but I do use my time on Monday and Tuesday quite efficiently to find Markus a real cat, buy Ryan an anniversary present, research the bands playing Coachella because I haven't heard of almost any of them before, play several hours of Civilization, and have a couple of online cam sessions with inexperienced but hot provincial girls from states I'd never step foot in.

The first thing that happens at work on Wednesday morning, as it does every Wednesday morning, is that the whole business grinds to a halt and everyone gathers around in a set area near the middle of the open plan office to participate in a company meeting. And by participate in a company meeting I mean stand there looking anything between bored and despondent, while Theo Rothchild delivers a grandiose lecture about 'business developments' and 'industry updates' from the past week. He refers to this as the Hump Day Huddle. Because, you know, he's down with the people. It's another of his magnificent innovations introduced when he was dragged in to torture us, and it's absolutely for the benefit of all employees and the well-being of the company and nothing to do with the fact that he's a deluded megalomaniac who loves the sound of his own voice and adores a subservient audience. The fact is that I'd forgotten this was happening today; otherwise I'd have worked from home again.

When we're finally released about forty-five minutes later, I'm simply too annoyed to do any work, so I sit at my desk and start searching online for famous Theos in history instead. My favorite one, and the one that seems most closely related to my current one, is Roman Emperor Theodosius I, ruler of the Roman Empire at the end of the 4th century. I read up on him on Wikipedia and email Kurt:

'Oh my God, look, it's history repeating:

"Theodosius I, also known as Theodosius the Great, was Roman Emperor from 379 to 395. Following his ascension to the throne, his reign was marked with internal strife within the Empire. A career soldier with little knowledge of statecraft, Theodosius wisely surrounded himself with trusted advisors. He issued decrees that effectively made Christianity the official state church of the Roman Empire. In 393, he banned the Olympics in Ancient Greece. It was not until the 19th century, in 1896, that the Olympics were held again."

You just need to replace a couple of words and these guys have led parallel lives:

"Theo Rothchild, also known as Theo the Cunt, was Managing Director from 2012 to [unspecified]. Following his ascension to the ergonomic kneeling chair, his reign was marked with internal strife within Neon Sphere. A Business School charlatan with little knowledge of how to actually run a business, Theo soon found himself surrounded by numerous, albeit powerless, enemies. He issued decrees that effectively made the Hump Day Huddle the designated time of the week to take a look at your life and start asking some serious questions about who you are, how you got there, where it all went wrong. In 2012, he banned getting any enjoyment out of your work in Neon Sphere. It wasn't until [unspecified] when Theo was forcefully removed for crippling the company's profitability that any enjoyment was gotten again."

I'm not kidding when I say that I truly believe our Theo to be Theodosius' reincarnation. What do you think?'

Kurt writes back:

'I just had a look online and I can't find anything in Roman history about the Emperor garishly repainting the palace in a self-important rage, otherwise the stories are too similar. Also, were the rooms in the palace inexplicably named after types of fruit and vegetables?'

'Yes, of course. You do know that the original name for the Colosseum was The Strawberry Guava, don't you? And it was painted a shocking shade of fire engine red from floor to ceiling. Well, they didn't have fire engines then so they didn't call it that, also the Colosseum has no ceiling, but you know what I mean.

Anyway, have you had sex with anyone in the grape room today so far?'

'No, not yet. Although, now that you mention it, Tina Underwood from HR is looking really HAWT today and she would be my number one choice right now.'

'I'm sure she would be. She was just emailing me actually. She revealed that Gino from IT support heavily flirted with her when he went over to fix her wi-fi connection for her, and – shock horror – she actually enjoyed it. Despite him looking the way he does. Women are weird.'

'I see. Does she email you a lot?'

'Not really, calm yourself down. Maybe once a week or so, about fun stuff anyway.'

'She's a cold bitch, isn't she?'

'Yes. Only Gino has been able to penetrate her ~~frosty exterior~~.'

'We'll see about that. What about you? Any erotic developments in the office?'

'Well, you see Kwasi has been overly friendly towards me recently. I have to say, I would totally be up for it, just because we have this special bond anyway. And based on the rumors circulating that he's a very considerate and sensual lover, of course.'

'Good call. Let me remind you that the cherry room is there for gay play anyway, so someone has to use it. Please keep me informed.'

When I'm done in the office, I drive back home and pick up Markus and we're off to collect this cat that he's buying. His current mood is a bit more subdued than I would have expected, although this might have to do with the fact that we have to drive to Lancaster, north of the city, for this transaction to take place. I'm not exactly sure where he was expecting people whose main profession is 'cat breeder' to be living. When we get there, the house looks like a lifeguard hut having gone through a mild typhoon. I reckon that possibly at some point in the past it was painted a vibrant turquoise, but all that's left of that now is the occasional flake of color on the disheveled wooden boards that make up the exterior. The front yard cleverly serves a dual purpose: both suburban jungle and large-scale trashcan. Kinda feel like we need to rescue this little cat as quickly as we can and get the hell out of here. Thankfully, the woman who answers the door has a similar idea. We step into a filthy living room filled with cat toys, scratching posts and heavily marked furniture and are told to wait. She disappears behind a closed door into another room, seemingly populated by a very loud TV, an old man with a persistent cough and a litter of three-month old Russian Blue kittens. This indicates to me that the house has other rooms even more disgusting than the one we're standing in and I should be grateful. Less than a minute later the cat lady is back with a tiny grey cat in her arms. He looks startled. Markus melts, hands over a pile of cash to her and we're gone.

'I'm going to name him Frost,' he says. 'After the experimental musician Ben Frost and also the Björk album track from Vespertine, Frosti. Well, it's either Frost or Pertanimas. What do you think?'

'What's that?'

'What, Pertanimas?'

'Yes.'

'Cat's name.'

'If those are the only two choices, I'd go with Frost.'

'OK. Frost it is.'

'Good for you. Frost, the little Russian Blue cat. I like it.'

His cat is pretty damn cute; I'm not going to lie. The name is expectedly dumb.

When we get back to Markus' apartment, Frost finds comfort underneath the living room sofa and refuses to come out despite our determined attempts to lure him out with succulent roast chicken-flavored kitten and junior food specifically designed to provide proactive nutrition to cats aged 1-12 months, specially formulated milk that helps promote a healthy kitten, a slice of prosciutto, and a number of toy mice (both squeaky and non). He's also so far back that we can't reach him sticking our whole arms down there whilst laying on the floor, so having run out of options, we leave him be.

Ryan's also come over to participate in the fun, as well as to organize

Coachella, which is now in two days. Unfortunately, she happens to already be killing my buzz, because she wants to head there on Friday afternoon, meaning that we're going to miss almost the whole of the first day. If we actually make it there at all before the end, that is, seeing as we'll be stuck in the festival traffic alongside a few thousand other losers who decided to leave it last minute and set off 'after work'. I might be tempted to let her go ahead with her own plan and drive down with Markus on Thursday instead, like most sensible people will, but Markus has now decided to drop out and stay at home with Frost. I should have found him a cat to buy next week instead.

Now, the other thing is that, over the weekend we're meant to be staying at Party Boy Michael Murphy's house in Palm Springs, but Ryan has this thing where she kinda hates Michael Murphy. Possibly even more than she hates most of my other friends, that is. A lot of it has to do with him being the kind of person who would have the nickname Party Boy. In fact, *all* of it has to do with that. Michael Murphy is partly unemployed / partly a DJ and I don't think he has seen the morning side of midday for the best part of the last decade. These facts alone are enough for Ryan to write him off as a human being. I tell her that if she doesn't want to spend the weekend there, perhaps she should recommend some of her own friends that we can stay with. Shockingly this doesn't appear to be an option, and we go with the original plan.

12

'The sunglasses you're wearing do not exist.'

That's the first thing that anyone tells me when we walk into Michael Murphy's house in Palm Springs on Friday evening. It's in one of those cul-de-sacs that a lot of middle-aged couples from Los Angeles keep in the desert for their retirement. In fact, this is Michael's parents' house as one can tell by the décor, which brings together brass, geometric mirrors, flowery lampshades and pastels in a combination last seen in Angela Lansbury's *Murder, She Wrote* house. The antiquated interior is counteracted by a number of young people who are having some very modern fun times indeed. OK, the music that's playing loudly from the speakers is modern, I suppose people did get drunk and jump around in swim suits back in the late 80s / early 90s too. It would seem that quite a few of Michael's friends decided to skip the first night of the festival and party at the house instead. The front door was half open, so I knocked somewhat pointlessly – no one could have heard it over the music – and we just went in.

I put my sunglasses on as soon as we drove up to the house and I heard there's a party going on. It just seemed like a very Coachella weekend thing to do. Ryan has already asked me to remove them twice in the time it took to park the car and walk up to the front door. She's now targeting her derision on the girl who's talking to me. The girl seems quite drunk. She's wearing a pair of striped blue men's boxer shorts and a yellow bikini top. Her body is hot. Her face is above average, slightly let down by a relatively flat nose and dull eyes, although the latter might just be the effect of the alcohol.

'What do you mean?' I say to her, smiling.

'Matte black Wayfarers don't come with black lenses. The sunglasses you're wearing do not exist,' she repeats.

'Are you saying that these sunglasses are merely a figment of my imagination?'

She laughs.

'Matte black Wayfarers only come with crystal green lenses or blue mirror ones. Never with black.'

She's now touching the side of my face with her free hand – the other one holding a plastic cup filled with some liquid – reaching for my sunglasses. She really is very curious about this.

Having failed to make the girl drop dead with her eyes, Ryan now decides to interrupt and says that we should go get a drink or find Michael and let him know that we're here. I remind her that I don't drink, and that Michael probably doesn't care. Regardless, she pulls me away just as soon as I've had the chance to find out the girl's name (Claire) and tell her that I'm looking forward to finding out more about sunglasses and possibly other accessories from her over the weekend.

We wander into the kitchen, where a small group of five or six people are doing tequila shots. I indicate to Ryan that perhaps this might be a good way for her to relax, and thankfully she agrees. We walk up to them and say hi. Everyone appears to be extremely friendly. Everyone wants to get us in on the shots. I say that I don't drink, but I'm sure that my girlfriend would love to play. Telling people that you don't drink is the quickest and easiest way to get inundated with alcohol offers. People just find it incomprehensible that anyone wouldn't drink, especially by choice, without having what's perceived to be a 'valid' reason. The range of 'valid' reasons is quite narrow, really just incorporating two: a) being a recovering alcoholic and b) having been involved in a tragic, alcohol-related car accident where at least a life or someone's mobility was lost. Deciding not to drink without any previous life-shattering personal experience is simply unacceptable. Most of the time people refuse to let me off without putting up a good fight, and insist that tonight should be the night when I'm going to have my first drink, when I'm going to become a new person, discover a whole new world I've been sheltered from so far. I hear all this every time I meet someone new, and of course it's never worked. I don't mind people's tenacity though. It doesn't really annoy me, no more than most other human traits anyway.

Ryan has her shot and picks up a cocktail from the kitchen counter. I get a bottle of water from the refrigerator and we walk out through the back door. I'm disappointed to see that there's no swimming pool.

Michael Murphy is out there sitting on the small wall separating the patio from the back garden, having a cigarette. Three of his friends from LA that I know are there with him. These must be the people who are staying at the house this weekend. I really don't know where the other twenty-five people in the house came from.

'Great party, Michael Murphy,' I say. 'We're here at last.'

He sits up and gives Ryan and me both a bear hug. Not separate bear hugs, there's no need – we both fit in the same one. Michael is pretty gigantic in physical size, as well as mannerisms. I once did spend an afternoon looking up bear species online, just to see which one he's most like. Turns out he's a combination of your typical North American black bear (judging by his mild temperament) with the looks of a terrifying grizzly. Like all bear species, however, he's mostly nocturnal.

'Parke, bro! You finally made it. Ryan, always nice to see you.'

Ryan's tequila shot has helped her enough not to be repulsed by him and she even offers:

'Thank you, Michael. Thanks for letting us stay.'

'No problem at all. Anything for my bud, Parke, here.'

I didn't know that we were buds necessarily, but he's letting us stay at his house plus we just got these hugs, both signs indicating to me that we probably are. I'm actually a little suspicious as to why he chose to waste one of the precious four bedrooms in the house on Ryan and me this weekend, but I suppose we got this gig through being Markus' friends. Markus and Michael hang out quite a lot because they're both massive pot addicts complete with those marijuana prescriptions they just hand out to everyone in California 'for medical reasons' these days. When Markus pulled out, I guess he was stuck with us.

Despite being slightly drunk, Ryan hasn't lost her control freak touch and wastes no time in asking Michael which one our bedroom is, so we can move our stuff in from the car. After that's done she allows herself to let her hair down, which is a bit of a relief.

This turns out to be a typical LA party with the exact same people you'd find in a Hollywood mansion on any given Thursday night, simply transported 100 miles southeast. I have lost count of the times in the past year when some ambitious nobody was introduced to me at a social event and launched into a practiced self-promotional tirade within seconds of our initial greeting. It literally goes: 'Hi my name is Stella Delgado, I'm a singer, *eeeef IIIIIIII, shouuld staaay, I would ooohnly be in your waaaaaeeaaaayyyyyy*'. It doesn't matter that I have no power or interest in promoting their showbiz career, all that matters is that I'm one more person that can be exposed to their God-given talent, and this is clearly a game of numbers. There are potential fans everywhere; you just have to find them and assault them into liking you. In ascending order of how disgusting I find them, I would place the main showbiz offenders thus:

5) Singers
4) Dancers
3) Models
2) Writers
1) Actors

Singers are tolerable, especially those that can sing. At least it's a skill that's objectively identifiable; you either can carry a tune, or you can't. It's still very peculiar though when people break into song inches from your face to advertise their talent. And this happens a lot. The most traumatic of these incidents took place at a Christmas party in this house in West Hollywood last December. I was walking around the garden talking to people with Ryan, when we were introduced to this vaguely Hispanic girl who very keenly presented herself as an up-and-coming singer. Ryan made the fatal mistake of asking her in a good-humored manner, 'Yes, but can you actually sing though?' which she took as her cue to move as close to me as she could, stare into my eyes and deliver two full verses and the chorus from 'Someone Like You' by Adele. I didn't know where to look. I fixed a grin on my lips and just stood there being sung to, attempting to trick my brain into self-imposed sensory deprivation. Cursed by bad timing, when the song finished we were ambushed by the party photographer, who proceeded to take a group shot of me, Ryan, the singer, and her so-called manager, an anemic-looking, albeit exceptionally loud, little English guy with a forced Californian intonation. A few days later, when this humiliating picture was uploaded on Facebook and we were all tagged, I clicked through to discover that 'Vina Moreno' described herself in the following way on her Facebook fan page (to all of her 67 fans): 'Free spirit, singer/songwriter, raw vegan, spiritually motivated, holistic healer. Song is my Religion, Love is my Universe'. And that told me everything I needed to know, more so than a live, oversung rendition of an obvious ballad, which had only served to inform me that there are more vowels in the word 'you' than I had ever imagined.

Dancers are pretty harmless too. They're just regular people like the rest of us, only a lot more camp and susceptible to occasionally being taken over by the beat. All people want to express themselves somehow. These particular people want to express themselves through formation dancing. The dancer's best opportunity to make you cringe comes in the gym. Very frequently when I go to train, I will be faced with random individuals succumbing to public displays of rhythm. Not just a little foot tapping or head nodding to the sound of their iPod, but properly breaking into short bursts of choreography. I'm still not sure whether, like singers, they feel the need to audition for everyone all the time, or whether this is a physical need forcing them to surrender, forget about everyone around them and DANCE!

Noticeably more annoying are models. I have to say, models are some of the weirdest people that exist. Being weird isn't a bad thing in itself, of course. But with models I mean *bad* weird. I reckon that deep down they're ashamed of what they do, so they develop all these personality quirks to give themselves substance. Most of them have other amazing interests and talents too, you know. Like, they're into molecular science or they make oil paintings of swans, etc. They're not *just* models, duh. I've never met a model who's just happy being a model and hasn't tried to sell themselves as something else at the same time. My two favorite models that I know are a girl called Joan Sui Ju and a guy called Tyler Kershaw. I have the misfortune of being Facebook friends with both of them. Joan is 26, which means 140 in model years, but she's still hanging in there. What I find most infuriating about her are the constant posts about politics and science, which intersperse her shots of pouting seductively from the floor of abandoned warehouses and doing star jumps contorting her body in such a way that her wrist is pointed at the camera so that we see whatever watch she's paid to advertise. Perhaps this is a personal failing, but I will never look to someone who's always made a living lying in underwear on car hoods for serious political debate. Tyler is even worse, because he's a man and he's 31. Tyler's way of throwing dust in our eyes about his actual worth as a human being is relentless posting of his art. This art comprises basic charcoal drawings of unattractive or ageing people, which definitely prove to me that Tyler is very deep and tormented and finds beauty in the most unexpected places, OK? Tyler is gay but looks down on the shallow queens who 'waste their lives going out, partying, drinking and sleeping with each other' (according to a recent status update of his) but not on the five nights a week when he's working behind the bar at The Locker Room in WeHo to supplement his income.

Writers come in at no.2 of infuriating types, because they probably have the highest opinion of themselves, on average. In a town where everyone is desperately trying to make it and is explicitly using his or her appearance to do so, writers take the high ground: they're better than other showbiz folk, because they're smarter. This is, of course, relative, because I really don't know how much intellect is required to outsmart your average TV show back-up dancer or Sunset Boulevard billboard model. More importantly, even for regular, outsider people like me it's virtually impossible to have a conversation with an aspiring writer. With every sentence, in every response, they're trying to land a punchline. You might as well just stand there and let them deliver their pre-conceived dialogue all by themselves; they're planning to do that anyway. A writer talking to another writer, however, is the pinnacle of pretension and embarrassment for everyone involved. It's the exact Los Angeles equivalent of two buck-deer sparring in the middle of a forest, only a lot less civilized. Writers like to think they're pretty good with words and as it happens, words are the medium we communicate in. If somehow the human race suddenly degenerated and primarily communicated through the medium of dance, I'm sure that dancer-on-dancer interaction would be the most competitive and cringe-worthy and I would be inclined to revisit my showbiz types ranking. As things are, writers retain the runner up spot.

Nothing can beat the champions of being unbearable though: actors. Meeting an actor is exactly as if you're meeting someone who proudly and explicitly states: 'Yes, I have a severe personality / mental disorder, which requires that I be adored and applauded at all times'. These people make a living, no, actually a *life* (because acting is never simply a job) out of demanding constant attention. Given my family background, it actually really surprises me that I'm not psychologically damaged enough to have gone down the acting path. Seriously, how much neglect must you have experienced in your childhood to crave this sort of adulation in your adult life? The worst of this group are the 'self-aware' ones, those actors who pretend they recognize the personality shortcomings of their chosen profession and the fact that they come across pretty badly to everyone who's heard the 'aspiring actor' story a few too many times. This is an increasing number in our time, when most people are quite savvy and tend to adopt a 'meta' approach when dealing with well-identified clichés. That is, more and more actors will claim awareness of 'how vain the whole endeavor' is and 'how many people are trying to make it', in an attempt to distance themselves from the ambitious, desperate masses who emigrate to LA to pursue their futile dreams. I was talking to this actor guy at Tommy Gillman's birthday dinner once, who went as far as to say that when people asked him what job he does, and to avoid the thespian stigma, he always replied that he's a janitor. Because, you know, he's not like the others. I took a look down at the table and commented: 'A janitor with such pretty actor hands?' He didn't speak to me for the rest of the evening.

A few people in Los Angeles unfortunately combine more than one of these top 5 showbiz vocations, which only results in increasing their annoying factor exponentially. Singer / dancer and model / actor hybrids are really quite common and you eventually learn to live with them. Other combinations are more difficult to stomach. There is, in fact, one particular guy that I know who self-identifies as a writer / model / actor. Somehow, bringing together those three talents has created some sort of chemical reaction making him more smug, conceited and self-absorbed than the individual parts would imply. Then again, this guy does have a Greek background, apparently, just like my father, which I find explains many of his shortcomings already.

13

I wake up around 1pm on Saturday afternoon after a good ten hours of sleep. Somehow I needed that. The only people left in the house are Ryan and another of the girls staying here for the weekend whose name I don't remember and who has made herself sick from drinking too much last night and doesn't feel like doing anything today. There is a certain cleverness to the idea of arriving somewhere early, starting to drink/take drugs early, collapsing early, and leaving early, but really, some people need to learn to pace themselves for a three-day long festival.

Ryan pretends to be exasperated and surprised that I've slept through the loud music that was playing all morning before everyone left, I ask her if she's met me before, I get dressed and we go out to get some breakfast, possibly lunch, because there's nothing in the kitchen at this place apart from half-empty bottles of alcohol and discarded plastic cups. Also, lots of ice.

Driving around the empty streets of whatever Palm Springs suburb we have the misfortune to be staying in in this unforgiving sun for the best part of half an hour trying to find somewhere semi-decent to eat, leads us both to a suspicious diner and the conclusion that there's nothing good about this god damn city. Honestly, if Palm Springs is the first thing that global warming takes down, and this is very likely, it will be nobody's loss.

Following this meal of deep-fried everything with a side of sorry looking disintegrating fruit, we drive over to the day's next ubiquitous desert cul-de-sac to attend a pre-festival party. I'm starting to wonder whether we'll actually attend any festival during the festival weekend. This party is much better than the one at our place last night, simply by virtue of the house having a swimming pool and the décor having received several updates since 1989. There are maybe forty people here, including everyone from LA that we'd made those initial plans to come here with. The presence of Jeremy, Rae, Tommy, Katie and everyone else from that group has an contrasting effect on me and Ryan, but at the end of the day, I don't recall the last time Ryan wasn't grumpy about something, so whose fault is that?

As is the case in most parties I go to, I have no idea whose house this is or how my friends and I ended up there. Demographically, the group here is very mixed, making it almost impossible to draw any useful conclusions about the person who gathered them all here. There are 20-something kids from LA, there's a handful of overly groomed middle aged women with deep tans who look like poorer versions of Orange County housewives, and there's a large number of muscular gay men in their 30s with their shirts off. The sum of all these parts would lead me to believe that the house belongs to a formerly married couple in their 50s who came to a messy divorce two or three years ago when the wife walked in on the husband giving a blow job to the Mexican gardener just in this pool house right here where the barbecue is set up. They've since developed forced friendly terms, mostly for the sake of their son, who's moved to LA for college but frequently visits back home to spend time with his old friends. The ex wife now spends her time bitterly bitching with her girlfriends over endless glasses of gin, while the ex husband boastfully flashes his new lifestyle and the men that came with it in front of her eyes. I have no evidence whether any of this is actually true. I probably need to start drinking or something.

Ryan is determined not to have any fun and wants to drag me down with her, so she imposes a rule that we have to leave for Coachella no later than 4pm. This gives us a staying time at this party of approximately forty-five minutes. Conversation quickly turns to how everyone is actually planning to get to the festival – apparently this is more difficult a task than anyone could have ever imagined. It's so late in the day that driving there would be quite pointless, and would lead to getting stuck in endless queues of cars circling the festival site waiting to get in limited parking lots that have already run out of space. The only other option is to walk there. The consensus from the bunch of obviously drunk people who don't know exactly where we are with relation to the festival that make up my friends is that this walk should take no longer than half an hour, and I'm happy with this assessment, so I'm willing to believe them. Ryan has a different idea, however, and enforces a 'we're leaving right NOW' policy, which I manage to ignore for about a quarter of an hour by hiding from her with Jeremy and Katie, before having no other option but to answer her calls, succumb and depart. None of the people we know want to leave yet, so Ryan and I set off on our own. In fact, the only others leaving the party at the same time are a group of middle aged gay bears, fully equipped with accessorized bicycles (pink paint, glittery mirrors, tassels, flower baskets) as well as outfits (pink body paint, glittery mirrored sunglasses, moustaches, fairy wings). I ask them for directions to Coachella, they laugh at my face when I mention we're planning to walk there, and it only becomes clear about an hour later that, yes, perhaps I was the one looking more ridiculous at that point.

As it happens, this is a two-hour walk at least, definitely longer if we hadn't given up and taken up the offer of a Latino family in an SUV offering lifts to the festival entrance for $10 a head to lost, white dumb kids like us. When they drive us up there, I'm so happy and relieved that I shove a $100 bill in the father's hand before running out of the car to buy two 2-litre water bottles, which go a little way to relieving the severe dehydration we've been experiencing. I guess we'll have to deal with the third degree sunburn later. What's even worse, once we go in and walk around a bit, we spot our whole group of friends, who arrived there about an hour ago having just driven in and used the available parking space with very little effort. At this point I give Ryan an 'I told you so' look loaded with so much accusation that would surely give her a headache had she not been already suffering from heatstroke, she responds with her trademark 'oh, just grow up' eye daggers, and just like that, without saying anything at all, we decide to spend some time apart before this disintegrates into something even uglier. Sometimes I think it's so romantic that we manage to communicate like that without using any words.

Ryan walks off with the girls to have a look at the dance tent, and I go over to pick up a 21+ wristband with Jeremy, so that I can join Tommy and the other guys in the beer garden where they're drinking. Despite being only 23, it kinda feels to me that so many people in this place are very, very young. There seems to be a lot of fraternity douchebag action going on, plus countless girls who look like they're 17 and out to have a wild weekend away from their parents' house. I'm not even sure what the 21+ wristband rule is all about; everyone seems drunk. I suspect foul play via cooperation between two main pairs of socioeconomic groups: a) underage frat bros and 30-something gay guys, and b) teen girls and every straight male in his 20s. My theory is confirmed just minutes after I've received my wristband, when we get an entry-level hipster college girl in denim hotpants, a yellow shirt tied in a knot, and a pair of those new, inferior Wayfarers come up to us and flirtatiously ask if we'll help her buy a few drinks for her and her friends.

'I'll give you the money now, honestly.'

'How old are you?' I ask.

'20.'

'Yeah, right!' I laugh. 'We'll get you the drinks, but you really shouldn't be drinking, you know.' I don't know why I'm being paternal all of a sudden. Is this my way of flirting with teens? If so, I should probably be worried.

We walk up to the nearest bar as Jeremy attempts some small talk:

'Who are you here to see today?'

'Frank Ocean. Do you like him?'

'Um, not really. He's just trying to be Prince.'

'I like how he fuses electronic sounds with R'n'B.'

'Isn't that very Prince?'

'Yeah. But isn't everything something?'

I pick up three vodkas with Red Bull, she tries to give me some cash, which I don't take, and I think that our job here is done, so we go over to find Tommy in the beer garden.

Within half an hour or so, Ryan comes back. It's too much being apart from each other, she says, she's not going to enjoy this festival without me, we both need to get over ourselves, apologize and move on. It's one of those rare moments when I have to agree. There are some hotter girls than her around, but who can be bothered with all that at the end of the day.

'I'm sorry I made us walk in the blazing heat for two hours,' she says.

'I'm sorry I wanted to kill you when we finally got here,' I reply.

This appears to be mutually satisfactory and just like that we've made up.

Coachella is really fun and you don't even have to be interested in any of the music or have the first clue about that bands that are playing to have a good time, which certainly helps my case. I'm certain this music festival isn't actually about the music at all. Sure, I get to stand in various tents and watch parts of people's sets for ten minutes at a time before one of my friends decides there's somebody amazing that we possibly couldn't miss playing somewhere else, but the end destination never seems to be as rewarding as the way there. The way there incorporates buying more drinks, becoming acquainted with random festival-goers, exchanging drugs with them, rolling around on grassy fields with old and new friends, taking pictures that nobody will want to see in the morning, plus some meaningless hookups.

I'd be lying if I said that, despite maintaining my usual sobriety in a field packed with 20,000 people who are off their faces, I wouldn't be interested in this meaningless hookups aspect of the experience. There's a certain Brazilian girl that's now hanging out with us called Ana (a name which I like as it dispenses with western conventions to present a leaner, more efficient spelling model) who I really wouldn't mind making out with right now. Ana's 22 and she is, of course, a model. Apart from her long, tan thighs and realistically enhanced breasts, I'm also a big fan of her back-story. She arrived in the States a couple of months ago and is now living here, sidestepping the notoriously impossible US immigration by somehow managing to acquire an O-1 visa for her modeling accomplishments. The O-1 is usually reserved for individuals with extraordinary achievement in the arts, of which now modeling is one, allegedly. Whatever. A few thousand dollars spent on lawyers and anyone can get in. And after five months of paper pushing and waiting around, the most difficult part of the process, Ana says, was the final step, a face-to-face interview at the US embassy in Sao Paulo, where she's from. Although her application had already been approved, the embassy official, a hardened American woman in her 50s who'd seen way too many unqualified losers and other trash sidestep the system over several years let Ana through, but not before making the interview a traumatic experience. Kinda feel like I need to support this girl, kinda feel like I need to make her feel welcome.

I propose some minor fooling around to Ryan, perhaps some three-way kissing, but she doesn't want to get involved. I come up with an alternative suggestion of some regular, two-way kissing between me and Ana (who's up for anything because she's a South American model who's in the country fraudulently after all, let's be fucking honest here) but this goes down even worse. I'm a little surprised. I was expecting the three Ecstasy Ryan has taken to have loosened her up a little and they possible have, but not to this extent. In fact, long before the night is over she's decides that we should go home and get some sleep. I point out that nobody's going home yet, not to mention that I'd really like to see her try to fall sleep while her eyes are darting around manically like they are at this moment. Regardless, we end up borrowing Michael Murphy's car and driving back to his place in the next half hour (Michael said he would get a lift from one of the others). Ryan initiates sex – most likely because she's still high – and I go along with it despite really wanting to sulk at her, because she made us leave early. We both fall asleep soon after, Ryan having taken a couple of Valium.

I get woken up in the morning by some very loud packing. I'm guessing this is deliberate, because it really shouldn't be that laborious and noisy to put a couple pairs of shorts in a gym bag, so I take my cue and, half-asleep, mumble:

'What are you doing?'

'What does it look like? I'm packing.'

'Already? Aren't we leaving tonight?'

'No, I want to go now. Soon anyway. I have to work tomorrow.'

'Well, I thought we could go to the festival for a couple of hours this afternoon and then go from there.'

'You know that's not going to happen. We'll end up getting home very late.'

'Right. Well, do you mind if I stay?'

'Yes, I expected this. You can do what you like. Stay here and have fun with your amazing friends.'

'Yeah, I'm not sure what your problem is with them. You seemed to be having a good time with everyone last night.'

'I can tolerate them when I'm high on drugs, that's more or less it. I don't under normal circumstances like to spend any time around people like, say, Rae Prinz.'

'What's Rae ever done to you? She's not a bad person.'

'People say that about everyone. What is the actual threshold for making somebody a bad person? Does reckless homicide qualify you only? Rae makes people around her feel uncomfortable and treats those she doesn't consider as being in her "circle" with contempt. Pretty bad person behavior as far as I'm concerned.'

'You know, arguing about Rae Prinz is not what I want to be doing first thing in the morning. Especially with someone who's clearly undergoing a major comedown. Since you don't mind, I'll stay. I'll drive to LA with somebody later this evening. I'm really sorry you want to go back now, I know I won't have as much fun without you.'

'Yeah, right.'

'It's true. Well OK, I'll be back tonight. Or first thing tomorrow morning if I can't find anyone who's driving up tonight.'

14

When I get home on Wednesday after seven in the evening, I change into a pair of swimming shorts and head down to the pool. I swear it must be the warmest evening of the year so far. I can feel small drops of sweat forming in between my eyebrows underneath my sunglasses in the time that it takes to walk from the lobby round the building to the pool. Ryan is there. I'm not sure I expected this. She's sitting on the side with her legs dipped in the water, facing the way that I'm coming from. It looks like she's been expecting me. The only other person around is a heavily pregnant dark-haired woman in her early 30s that I've seen in the building once or twice before. She's lying on a lounger underneath an umbrella, avoiding the sun. I walk over to Ryan, take my shirt off and sit down next to her. She bends her left knee, bringing her leg out of the water and puts her arms around it, as she turns her head away from me. That's a funny way of greeting somebody you've been sat there waiting for.

I start this off with something innocuous before allowing her to bite my head off, as I imagine she's desperate to.

'Can't believe how hot it still is. I'm halfway in the water and I'm still sweating.'

'I'm surprised you stayed in the desert until now, if you hate the heat so much.'

I laugh nervously. 'Here we go…' I'm trying to be humorous, but I think she reads this as insolence.

'Seriously, where *have* you been for three days? What *were* you doing all this time?'

'Um, I was staying at Party Boy Michael Murphy's house. Like you were over the weekend, remember? I was just hanging out with those guys.'

'It's Wednesday.' Her voice is getting louder. I'm starting to get embarrassed for both of us. 'Don't these people have jobs to go to? Doesn't anyone you surround yourself with have a fucking job?'

'Oh we're swearing now, I see. Were you brought up to talk that way?

It doesn't surprise me.'

She pushes me back. I wasn't expecting this and the impact makes me fall back, landing on my elbow. Fuck, this actually hurts. I'd happily do the same were it not for the pregnant woman, who's pretending not to watch us behind her stupid oversized sunglasses.

'Have you lost your mind?'

'You were being an asshole. I'm sick of you and your vapid friends and the places where you go and the things that you do and the shallow little world that you've enclosed yourself in.'

'I'll take my world any day over your miserable job and your tragic white trash family.'

She slaps me really hard in the face. Did I deserve this? Probably. The woman across the pool hurriedly picks up her stuff and walks away. I sort of wish I could leave too, but I'm strangely engrossed by this fight. It's like a car crash that I have to keep watching, even though I'm actually in it.

'Shut the fuck up about my family.'

'I'm sorry, miss, you grew up on a farm, you say?'

'You know… whatever. At least my parents were there for me. At least I knew who my father was and at least my mother has always cared.'

'I think you should drop this right now.'

Calmly, and having found a way to get to me finally, she goes on.

'I know you've been hurt. I know why you're acting like a child. Like no one else matters in the world apart from you. Why you're psychotically self-involved. I can't imagine that anyone with your childhood would have turned out a different way.'

'When did you become a psychologist? Or does everyone develop great human insight when they reach your age?'

'See? Child. You can't take it out on me though. It wasn't my fault that you were robbed of your childhood. It's not my fault that you've only met your father twice and you have a mother that's equally absent despite her physical presence. You simply have never had a normal parent / child relationship, where you could be irresponsible, unaccountable, careless. And you're making up for all this by behaving like this now that you're an adult.'

'My mom has had her own problems, but there's never been a question on whether she loved me. She's always treated me well.'

'No, Parke. She hasn't. I've met her; I've seen her around you. Some people are not meant to have children. Your mother is one of them.'

I don't speak for a few seconds. I realize suddenly that I'm very thirsty. My throat feels dry and I have no words left to say, nothing that can make me feel better. I just need to drink some water.

'I don't want to be around you.' I get up, put my shirt back on and start heading to the main building.

'That's right, just walk away. This will solve all your problems.'

'I don't want to be around you,' I repeat. 'That's all.'

This doesn't faze her. 'You know, I was thinking, if on your drive here you'd crashed your car and had died somewhere...nobody would have cared. Not really. And you know why? Because people see no worth in you. And what's worse, is that neither do you.'

I walk away. She gets up and follows me.

It's quite clear to me that I don't want her to stay in this apartment tonight, maybe not any other night, and I tell her so. Realizing perhaps that some things do affect me after all, even though I have a really high threshold, she begins apologizing in an almost hysterical way. I don't get this girl. Does she want to be with me, or does she not? Does she want to be with me, but only if I were a different person? Does she think that if she stays long enough, I will turn into a changed version of myself that she finds acceptable? Or is she so scared to be alone that she'd rather stay in a mutually abusive relationship that's crushing her spirit little by little each day? These are all questions that, right now, I'm not interested in finding answers to. I just want to be as far away from her as humanly possible, something which she's making quite difficult standing there sobbing on my doorstep. The easiest way out of this miserable situation that I can see is to accept her apology and tell her that everything is OK, which I proceed to do in what seems to be quite a convincing way. Perhaps she wasn't looking for sincerity. We finish our evening with me fucking her in the shower, as initiated by her – I was only trying to wash nearly a week of desert off me when she walked into the bathroom – and I fall asleep next to her before the opening credits for whatever tedious old film she has chosen to watch in bed has even finished. I'm too tired for all of this.

When I wake up in the morning she's already gone to work. She's left a number of notes around the house – on the coffee maker, underneath the toothpaste, in my underwear drawer – telling me how much she loves me and wishing me an awesome day. I think those are designed to make me forget the fact she told me I should be dead less then twelve hours ago. I go over to Markus' and let the cat in his bedroom, which does a great job in waking him up within seconds by jumping on his head and biting his face. He seems quite aggravated, even more so than if I had woken him up myself. I bet that cat won't be around by the end of the month. I shout at him a little bit to make sure he's fully conscious and awake and make coffee for both of us in the kitchen.

'When did you get back?' he asks.

'Yesterday evening.'

'And how was it?'

'Awesome. Really awesome, actually. Was staying at Party Boy Michael Murphy's house. Several new people turned up on Monday, so I stayed a couple more days. I don't think I slept more than five hours on Monday and Tuesday night. I don't really know why I'm up now, to be honest.'

'Well, I'm glad someone was having a good time. Your girlfriend here was chewing my ear off for three days. She lives here now, by the way, right? This is official? Anyway, she was asking where you are, what you're doing, whether I've heard from you, why you're not answering your phone. Not sure in how many different ways I could tell her that I didn't know and I didn't care.'

'Um, yeah, about that. I'm kinda over that.'

'By "that", do you mean Ryan?'

'Yes.'

'Well, that's a development, I guess. Are you sure? She's pretty hot… for someone her age.'

'Ha, yes. Whatever. I don't see it anymore. Maybe just when I'm fucking her. In any case, I think she actually hates my guts. She certainly can't stand me. She sees the worst in me and is constantly dismissive. Whenever I'm around her, I feel so shitty about myself. I'm starting to believe that I'm good-for-nothing, spoilt, entitled and a complete loser.'

'But Parke…'

'Shut up.' I pause. 'You know, when I came back yesterday, she practically assaulted me. She shoved her boney little fingers into my chest and pushed me back, I landed on my elbow, then she told me I'd be better off dead and that no one would miss me. Come to think of it, she was probably drunk. Drunk people behave like that, I know that much.'

'That's a pretty cool story. What did you say?'

'Nothing. I just wanted to walk away.'

'OK. You know, first of all, you shouldn't feel bad about the person that you are, just because some redneck chick with an inferiority complex doesn't like it. Second of all, you need to end this.'

'I definitely think it's time for a break.'

'Forget the break. You have to dump her ass.'

'I'm not sure I can do that. Last night she went berserk when I said I didn't want to see her anymore. I think I'm safer suggesting a break. Then I can sneak away quietly and never talk to her again while she's not paying attention.'

'That seems like the Parke Hudson way, well done.'

'Thank you. So... I'm going to move to San Francisco for the summer. Coming?'

'That sounds quite perfect, actually. I'll only come for a few days, because, you know, I have a cat to take care of now.'

'Oh yes, sorry, I forgot. You're crippled down with responsibility at the moment.'

'When are you going?'

'Possibly at the end of May, beginning of June, I suppose. I'll talk to work about it today.'

'Great. I'll come with and stay for the first few days. We can ask Ryan to feed the cat while I'm there. It will make her feel involved.'

'Like she's still part of my life. Perfect.'

Later in the afternoon I drive to Tiffany and buy a $1,000 pearl necklace for her – this should help avoid hysterics when I break the news – before surprising her by picking her up from work when she's finished for the day. I've made a reservation at a restaurant called CUT in Hollywood, where I thought we'd celebrated a ridiculous six-month anniversary or something, on her insistence, I'm sure of it. Why would I choose to celebrate half-year anniversaries? When we get to CUT, it turns out that I was mistaken and she's never been to this place before. I really can't think who I ate here with. It doesn't matter. It's still a decent restaurant, even without the memories I had wrongly assigned to it. So decent, in fact, that it doesn't take Ryan long to question why I'm suddenly being so nice and what my motives are. I take this as the opportunity to get into the spiel I practiced with Markus earlier. I tell her that I love her more than anything and that I can see me spending the rest of my life with her. I tell her that we've been having a lot of arguments recently though and that this friction is causing unhappiness for both of us. I say that there's absolutely no way I want to end things, I don't think I could live without her, but the best thing for us to do would be to take a step back and refocus on our relationship, on the love that we have for each other, forgetting the small grievances, the small problems that everyday routine has recently caused. And the best way to do this is to put some distance between us, whilst maintaining our bond, our commitment to each other. I'm moving to San Francisco for a few weeks, I say. We'll talk every day and you can come visit if you like, maybe on a weekend, but being apart for a while will only be good for us.

She seems incredulous but I think realizes that she's better off letting me have this one, and maybe she even believes me, I don't know. I tell her that I'm leaving in a few weeks and give her the necklace that I bought. 'I want you to wear this every day and think of me,' I say. I add that pearls go with everything (just trying to be helpful as I can't imagine somebody with her socioeconomic background would know that) and we finally put an end to this evening, hopefully relationship.

15

My mother has been haunting the house I grew up in for several years, although she's not technically dead. She does, however, lead a mostly indoor life, floating from one room to another in a cloud of gin, self-pity and regret. I'm not sure if *living in the past* is a suitable phrase to describe her current state, as this would imply a thriving existence at some previous point. From what I understand, this woman has never demonstrated any signs of being alive give or take some basic biological functions like her heart pumping blood around her body and her lungs drawing and expelling air at regular intervals.

My mother, Sadie, was born in Hillsborough, CA, grew up in this very house and has occupied its extensive grounds for the best part of the last forty-five years. I believe that this so-called life of hers may have started off well, but as it happens the blissful, careless times didn't last very long – both my grandparents were killed in a car accident when she was no older than ten and she quickly lapsed into a deep depression that she's never been able to shake off. I suppose there's only so much you can draw from a mere decade of happiness that took place over thirty-odd years ago.

For a brief time in her 20s, mom relocated to London, where I suppose she expected to find a more welcoming climate for her grey, insipid mood. I went to London once and knowing what it's like now I find the fact that somebody with my mother's temperament didn't hang herself while she was there both truly shocking and enough to give hope to even the most tortured souls amongst us. If *she* didn't kill herself *there*, well… what *does* it take to stick that gun in your mouth, really? I believe she spent her years in London studying psychology. She has actually spent most of her years anywhere studying psychology and I'm not sure why she's not found the reason why she's so fucked up. Perhaps it's not written in a book. Perhaps she hasn't got to the right book yet.

Whilst in London, one of the most unfortunate events of my mom's already miserable life occurred. One might have thought that losing her parents during her childhood would have been a lifetime nadir, but then she went and met my father. It's unclear what brought together a misanthropic, depressive alcoholic and an embittered sociopath addicted to sedatives, but love does seem to find a way to grow in the murkiest places. This ill-fated affair lasted only a couple of years until Maine, for that is his name, unceremoniously decided to move to California and take up his drug addiction full-time. This was funded by his Greek / American family, who were also quite rich (still are?) though nowhere near my maternal grandparents' standard. I'm not convinced that mom was truly devastated when he left her like that, as it would require moments of clarity, sobriety and a pause from her obsessive introspection to take offense at something someone has done to her externally. Still, she had the good sense to move back to the States as soon as she realized that she was pregnant with his child. I can't even imagine the consequences of having been born in England. Perhaps neither could she. In any case, mom didn't even tell Maine about me until years later. By that time, he had ended up straight where he was heading before they even met – dropping in and out of rehab clinics on both sides of the Atlantic. They've only actually met a handful of times since their time in London – the most recent being almost ten years ago. I don't believe they're likely to ever meet up again. Despite having practically cut him out of her life, mom felt it was the right choice to pass his last name on to me when I was born: I'm officially a Hudson. This type of psychological self-harm on her part must be how all people with mental issues behave.

As for myself, I've only met Maine twice. The first time was when I was 16 and mom took me to London to see him at my insistence. He was in rehab. It was a lovely trip. I wish every teenage son could meet their dad for the first time under such circumstances. After that I pretty much stopped asking about him. I saw him again a couple years ago during a summer break from college back in San Francisco. He was out of rehab and was going through one of those delusional, optimistic spells that all addicts routinely experience, where they think they've kicked the habit and can turn their lives around before tragically relapsing again. He'd flown to San Francisco to try to force a meeting with mom. He never succeeded. I went to meet him instead, because I felt sorry for him. I wish I hadn't. He was such a fucking mess and seeing him in his uplifted, hopeful, almost manic state was even more depressing than our first meeting when he at least had the decency to acknowledge the situation that he was in. There's nothing worse than a spirited addict. This second time that we met, I felt like I could see through his lies, the lies he was telling me, as well as himself, and it made me sick. I'll never ever drink. I'll never touch any drugs. I'll never allow this person in my life.

It's a fine Friday evening when Markus and I touch down in San Francisco. I feel happier already having left Los Angeles, Ryan, everything behind. Mom's driver, the same guy she's employed for the last two decades and whose name escapes me, is there to pick us up. I greet him with a bear hug despite being perfectly aware that none of the long-term staff at the Hillsborough estate particularly like me – I was a bit of a nightmare growing up, though they should try having a childhood with unbounded privilege and minimal restraint and see how they fare. During the short drive from the airport back home Markus proceeds to get drunk (he wants to get a reasonable buzz to match my mom's before meeting her, he says) as I sit back and send numerous messages to old friends and acquaintances who are still in the city. I want everyone to know I'm back for the summer. I also update my Facebook page checking myself in in San Francisco and commenting 'THANK FUCK THAT I'M HERE' in all caps. By the time we get home, this post has resulted in two missed called from Ryan and three text messages where she's pretending to have taken it personally and be all hurt and upset, which isn't a bad outcome.

Despite having visited for the weekend only a couple of months ago, I've missed home. I realize this as we drive in from the road, under the tunnel that leads from the outside courtyard to the cobblestone area that the main house is facing. Boston, Los Angeles, they're all fun, but this is where I want to end up living for sure. We go in through the main entrance and are greeted by Denning, whose name I do remember as he's the closest I've had to a paternal figure whilst growing up, if somebody who serves you your breakfast, makes sure your laundry is always done and answers the door when your friends come visit can count as a paternal figure. Denning points me to covered patio at the back of the house, where mom's apparently sitting. I think that it might have taken a while, but I would have eventually found her on my own following the smell of her cigarette. It's a relatively clear, warm evening, but there's moisture in the air – despite not being able to see clouds in the sky, you can feel tiny, hardly-there drops surrounding your skin, like a thin veil of wet mist.

Mom's sitting on a black iron chair gazing out over the outdoor pool. The only light on the patio is the red glow of her cigarette. There's complete silence out here. When she hears us step out on the patio, she turns around and, with what must be immense effort, raises a smile and says 'welcome home, boys'. Her voice comes out strange, cracking in her first syllable, as though she hasn't said anything for a while. I wonder for how long. There's a bottle of gin on the table next to her, three quarters full. I'm guessing this was brought out to her some time in the last hour. Before Markus has even had the chance to enquire, Denning walks out with a glass of Scotch and places it on the table. Markus winks at him and takes a seat next to mom, who seems to have got lost again focusing on an unidentified point in the pitch-black horizon. Having had enough of this already, I go back inside the house and walk upstairs to my bedroom.

Everything's pretty much like it was when I lived here, although noticeably neater, cleaner and tidier, as if someone's maintaining this as a showroom. Walking in through the double doors from the corridor, the most striking feature is a kingsize four-poster bed audaciously placed right in the middle of the room, facing away towards the flat-screen TV attached to the single navy wall. All the other walls are painted a pale tint of off-white, which is almost exactly the same shade as most of mom's pearls – the one piece of jewelry she constantly wears in different variations – just in case her presence in the house wasn't prominent and enduring enough already. There is a white tufted armchair and a few dressers against two of these walls (the fourth wall is mostly taken up by windows) and in the far left corner of the room, next to the door leading to the bathroom, there's an antique mahogany desk with nothing but a Tiffany lamp and a brand new 27-inch iMac on it. Did they really just replace my previous model with the latest one even though I don't actually live there? A few mismatched, overlapping Persian rugs cover the biggest part of the pinewood floor. Not for the first time, it strikes me how little this looks like the room of a teenager, let alone a young child. The only light touch in this space is a model sailboat on one of the dressers that measures 50 inches in height from the base to the top of the mast (I know this because I finally got to be taller than my toy when I was ten years old) but even that is an antique rather than something you'd buy for your child to break. Who decided on the daunting old furniture? Who made the call that mahogany is a suitable childhood companion? Who, in fact, forgot that there was a child living here? There's only one answer to these questions course, of course, and she's gulping gin in the outdoor patio downstairs right now. I don't care all that much though. I like the room very much now that I've grown up and this must be all that matters.

16

I turn the computer on and call Ryan on Skype. She's at my house watching TV with her friend Reed and Markus' cat, a predicament that might actually be the source of all her problems. She makes a moderately sized scene about my San Francisco post while I try to defend myself saying that it had nothing to do with her or her beloved Los Angeles (she interrupts me to say she doesn't like Los Angeles, I just dragged her there) and I wrote what I did because I was glad to be back in my home city and looking forward to seeing my family, can she really begrudge me for that? We go around in a few circles about this until she eventually gets over it and decides to move on to the next point of contention for the evening: am I going out tonight and if so, why? I tell her that I'm too tired, probably not, she tells me that she misses me and wish she were there with me, I agree and we hang up.

I go downstairs to find that neither Markus nor mom has moved. Moreover, there's an intense smell of weed in the air. So proud.

Somewhere in his buzz, Markus finds the energy to ask me what we're doing tonight and I tell him that I'm not quite sure, but I'm definitely not sitting here to watch the pair of them get more and more wasted. So we have something to eat and we drive up to the city.

We first meet up with Davis, a friend from school, and the people he's just finished having dinner with outside this Italian restaurant in Hayes Valley. The group consists of the girl that he's currently dating, a suspiciously young sandy-blonde who introduces herself as 'Ryot with a y' and can, literally, be no older than 17, two of her girlfriends (not nearly as fuckable, also in their teens) a British guy called Lloyd that Davis is working with, and Lloyd's boyfriend. Davis dropped out of college in his second year, I think he was studying something to do with engineering, and created his own startup (funded by his parents, of course) down in Palo Alto. He's designed some app of some sort, and I have no doubt that at some point he will be very successful.

After all the girls and the gays in the group finish fawning over Markus we all drive over to the Mission to go to a bar called 33 Kicks, a name which I quite like, although I would definitely change it to 44 Kicks, because 4 is much better number than 3, any way you look at it.

It's nearly midnight now and just before we go in Ryan gives me a couple more missed calls, which I duly ignore. She then texts me informing me that she knows I've gone out, which reminds me that I need to disable this stupid phone tracking app that we both have, as it's only likely to get me in trouble. I don't want to infuriate her even further, plus it really bugs me when people don't like me, whether they have a good reason or not, so I call her back and say that yes, I have gone out because Markus wanted me to, plus Davis got in touch, but it doesn't mean anything and I'm constantly thinking of her. I add that we both have to be strong and we have to be patient and we need to give each other a bit of space, because I really want our relationship to work as much as she does, and this seems to be the best way to make it happen. She must be really desperate as she accepts that, apologizes for calling me too often, it's just that she's missing me, I tell her not to be silly and she can call me as often as she wants, we exchange 'I love yous' and hang up.

Markus who has stayed back with me and heard the whole conversation asks me if I really think this is the best way to deal with this, I tell him that I don't know if it's the best way, but it's my favorite one and we go in to join the others.

I can hardly believe they let the trio of underage girls in, but anyway, it happened and we meet everyone at the bar near the front. As Markus is getting in an argument with the bartender about the unsatisfactory range of Scotch options, and Davis chats to the ugly friends to pretend that he cares, I take the opportunity to acquaint myself better with Ryot. Ryot is 20 years old, apparently, and a writer. Upon further enquiry, it surfaces that she's also a promotional model. You know, like those people who stand outside parties and hand out gift bags. I've never met anyone who describes themselves as a writer first and foremost and actually makes their income from writing. Not here, not in LA, not in Boston. What's wrong with these people? Is being a writer the height of intellectual achievement? A lot of delusional, conceited underachievers out to impress appear to think so. Whatever. Ryot is originally from a small town near Palm Springs called San Jacinto plus she seems to really be into Davis, so I stop talking to her and suggest we all take a walk to find some seats or something, as I'm actually getting tired.

Seeing that Lloyd's boyfriend (name: Khaled) is the only other person apart from me that's not drinking, I assume that he's the designated driver within the couple and I make a passing, humorous comment about having to stay sober for his boyfriend. He looks at me indignantly and spits out:

'I'm staying sober for myself.'

Well, first of all I don't like anyone who doesn't drink at all. I know that I don't, but for some reason it just seems…suspicious when somebody else doesn't. I'm not sure I can trust them.

Secondly, I'm not sure quite what his answer means, my first guess is that I offended his religious sensibilities or something, so I turn to Davis and describe the incident looking for an explanation. The truth is better than one could ever have hoped. Khaled used to drink everything and take all the drugs, like a combination of both my parents, I suppose, until a fateful night in London about a year ago. London is very big for the gays and for drug taking and Khaled was living there, doing his post-grad at UCL. During one of his 48-hour partying weekends, he was out in a club, making the most of having no responsibilities via getting absolutely trashed. At some point, the unidentified white powder he snorted from the key that some acquaintance held underneath his nose turned out to be ketamine. Ketamine can have the effect of creating hallucinations, the illusion of detachment from one's body and other fun experiences like that. During his ketamine incident, Khaled went somewhere really weird with his mind and had what he describes as an epiphany. Was it pure hallucination, did he go through a portal and connect with a different dimension, the scientific details remain unclear. The point is that when Khaled came out the other side of his episode a new man, someone who doesn't need the artificial effects of alcohol or drugs to experience life to its full. In other words, he became a pseudo-spiritual, sanctimonious dick. I decide to avoid Khaled for the rest of the evening.

I make my way to the restroom. The corridor that takes you there is really quite narrow to the point where only one person can go through at a time. So I wait for a couple of people who are coming the opposite way to go past and then when I'm bored of waiting I step in, kinda forcing the next guy who's coming my way to stop and wait for me. As soon as I've walked past him he barks 'you're welcome' in an annoying passing-aggressive way with his dumb fake homie accent, so I turn around and say 'I didn't say thank you' just to get on his nerves some more. He shakes his head at me and walks away. At that moment a girl who must really like assholes and has overheard this exchange as she's coming out of the bathroom lets out a big laugh at my rudeness, so I grab the opportunity and stand in front of her blocking her way before asking:

'My name's Parke, who are you?'

'I'm Melanie,' she says.

'Melanie', I say. 'You appear to be a stranger. I'm partial to strangers. Let me buy you a drink.'

Melanie walks with me to the bar where my friends are standing and lets me buy her a drink. She doesn't seem concerned with telling any of the people she's here with that she's decided to abandon them for a random guy she picked up outside the bathroom; if she's here with any people, that is. Her eagerness and instant availability make me respect her very little, if at all, and that's something that's really turning me on at this moment. Melanie is below average in height, even though it might be representative of her ethnicity, which I'm arbitrarily putting down as Cuban, has medium-length shiny brown hair held up in a high ponytail and the artificially blinding white smile of a health club receptionist that looks out of place on her peasant face. On the plus side, she does have a shapely ass and the right size of breasts for my liking. Behind her back, Markus is pulling some lewd faces (something puerile with his tongue inside his cheek) whilst at the same time giving her the thumbs down with both hands. Despite these mixed messages, I decide to press on.

It's now just after 2am. My phone rings. It's Ryan. I don't pick up, return the phone to my pocket and instead put my hands on Melanie's waist. She doesn't even pretend to flinch. With a full audience of Davis, Ryot, Lloyd, Khaled and the rest of them behind me, I start kissing her. I think I'm enjoying this on some level. There's a tap on my shoulder. When I pull away and turn around I see that it's Markus. I wave him away and go back to kissing this person. She seems to be getting into it quite a bit. It's not long before she moves her hands down to my hips and forces my body against hers. In order to make up for the difference in height I sit on a stool that's behind me and pull her close to me, inside my legs. Just a few seconds later Markus bugs me again, trying to properly pull me away. I stand up and ask him what the hell his problem is. He says that he doesn't think I should be doing this, seeing that I'm pretending to Ryan that nothing's wrong. I ask him whether he's had an epiphany of some sort, Khaled-style, and tell him to leave me alone. He says that perhaps there's a line somewhere that I shouldn't cross and I tell him to fuck off. Still, I only kiss Melanie for another minute or so, we exchange numbers, and I leave the bar with Markus.

On the way home Ryan calls once again and this time I answer. Why isn't she in bed?

'Baby! Why aren't you in bed?' I ask.

'I am. I just couldn't sleep.' She pauses. 'I was thinking about you. About us.'

'Don't worry, baby. We're alright.'

'You went out late, didn't you?'

'Yeah, just to this bar with Markus. On our way home now.'

'It's fine. I really don't mind.'

I can hear she's really struggling with this.

'You shouldn't. Nothing happened. It was fun. Markus had a couple of drinks. We hung out with Davis and some of his friends. I'm so tired, baby. Can I call you tomorrow? I wish I was there lying in bed with you.'

'Me too. Goodnight. I love you.'

'I love you.'

Markus tells me that I'm a complete dick, I tell him that I don't like him post his epiphany and we're back at home.

He stays out to share a joint with Manny, which is what our driver is called as I find out, and I go upstairs to take a late night shower. The whole corridor is covered in darkness, apart from a thin strip of light coming from underneath my mother's bedroom, four doors down from mine. I use that and the glow from my cell phone to find the way to my room. I quickly undress discarding my clothes on the floor as I walk into the bathroom. I let the warm water run over me, watching it run in streams through the hairs on my chest, my stomach and down to my legs. Damn, I'm horny. I wish I had taken that girl home to fuck. Actually not here. I wish I had fucked her somewhere else. I cut my shower short so that I can look online for porn, but by the time I'm in bed and playing on my iPad, I'm feeling too tired and quickly check emails and Facebook before turning it off and closing my eyes. Within seconds, in my state of semi-consciousness, I hear my bedroom door opening slowly and sense the movement of a person walking towards me. Sadie climbs under the covers into bed with me and puts her hand on my lower abdomen as I'm lying on my back. I'm suddenly wide-awake.

17

When I wake up in the morning, I find myself lying in bed alone. It's really quite early, just after 10 o'clock, but I can't sleep anymore. I take another quick shower, making it my third in the last eight hours, and go downstairs to eat. According to Denning, neither mom nor Markus are up yet, which totally figures. With nothing else to do I go back to my room and start playing *Civilization*. It's at least a couple of hours before Markus comes knocking on my door, being his usual groggy, incoherent early day self. His main focus this afternoon is his cat, so he makes us FaceTime Ryan just to check on Frost, his levels of fluffiness, adherence to meal times, playfulness, etc. Unfortunately the cat is hiding in his favorite spot, underneath the living room sofa, and we don't get to see him at all, so instead I am treated to Ryan's needy, terrified face and her incessant questions about the previous night, our plans for the rest of the weekend and the well-being of my mom, all of which seem like pointed questions with an ulterior motive to me, and I don't even consider myself to be a particularly suspicious person overall.

When this is done, we decide that we're hungry and drive over to Burlingame to get some lunch. On the way there, I beg of Markus that we talk about something else other than his cat, and if I were religious I would be taking this for an act of God, because he actually takes note and changes the subject to something that concerns me instead.

'So tell me,' he says. 'What kinds of things would you like to do, see, experience while you're here this summer? If you don't have an exact itinerary or specific plan in mind, feel free to use any noun, verb or adjective that seems remotely fitting.'

'What a great game,' I say. 'I guess I don't have an exact itinerary or specific plan, so I *will* put together a list of random nouns, verbs and adjectives. Like a "mood board" of sorts.'

'What's a "mood board"?'

'Exactly what you just described.'

'Oh.'

'Let me think:
Sea
Driving
Making lists, tearing them up
Interaction with locals
Running
Running
Movies
Seagull
Live band
A building burning down
Some rain.'

'This is very useful. I think we've made real progress here.'

'Yes, I'm glad my summer plans are now 2% figured out.'

'Where can we go eat now? You're kinda driving around aimlessly.'

'I know. Let's go to this place called Citizen down on Hillside. Davis mentioned it last night.'

'Citizen is a ridiculous name for a restaurant, but let's go anyway and I can blame you.'

The most important thing that happens at Citizen is that our waitress is young, cute, has a spark in her eyes and is currently hitting on us. Well, OK, she's hitting on Markus first and I'm waiting for my turn when he eventually weirds her out.

'That's an interesting tattoo,' she says, pointing at his forearm.

'Thanks...I think.' His people skills are really quite something.

'It's a cover up of something, isn't it? What did you have there originally?'

'It is, yeah. This was a humbling experience, actually. I had this really elaborate koi fish design. There was a beautiful, bright orange koi fish with golden highlights and these lively green eyes swimming upstream in a mass of deep blue, foamy water, its body twisted as it was struggling to overcome the rolling waves. You know, like I was struggling to overcome adversity.'

'Wow. I totally get that. What adversity were you struggling to overcome?' she asks.

'You see, that's the thing...what's your name?'

'Valerie. What's yours?'

'I'm Markus. And this is Parke. You see, Valerie, here's where the humbling part comes in. So I had my koi fish on me and I was feeling all defiant and brave and then I happened to see this homeless guy down at the soup kitchen in El Sereno in Los Angeles where I volunteer sometimes, who had the same tattoo. I mean, the exact same one. Maybe some color variations, plus his also had a few lotus flowers floating in the water, but other than that, identical. And I thought to myself, Valerie, oh...my...God. How can I stand here, serving this poor guy soup, thinking that I've had a hard time and that I'm overcoming adversity, swimming upstream like a beautiful koi fish, just because I went through a difficult break up with my ex who just wanted to use me for sex, when there are people out there who really are struggling and need to draw inspiration and strength from somewhere, even if it is just from the tattoo of a beautiful koi fish swimming upstream? I was just so embarrassed. I had my koi fish covered only days after that, and I've never looked back. Well, I look back when somebody asks me about the tattoo like you just did, but only with shame and regret.'

Sometimes it's nice to be present when these tattoo stories are told, because I can make an instant connection with the person that happens to be on the receiving end each time, if that's what I want. On this occasion that is exactly that I want, so I look up to Valerie, widen my eyes and purse my lips in a way that says 'Yup, I know' and suddenly I've got her full attention instead.

'I don't have any tattoos at all,' I say. 'Covered or uncovered. Can I possibly have your number though?'

'Don't you live in LA, as well?'

'No. I'm here for the next few months.'

She smiles at me, writes down her number on a napkin like we're in a 90s teen movie, gives Markus a look of disbelief implying that he's a complete madman, which isn't unfair, and walks away to carry on with her orders.

'There you go. You can thank me now, if you like,' Markus says.

'Yeah, because you came up with all that shit to alienate the hot girl so I could have her.'

'No, not deliberately, but it happened.'

'Thanks.'

'You should still break up with Ryan, if you're going to do all this.'

'Thanks, I'll think about it.'

After lunch we go back home and spend most of the day sitting by the outdoor pool. Markus is smoking weed, of course, and I do a few laps. There are times when he also jumps in for a swim, and that might have been careless and unsafe for somebody else in his current state, but Markus operates best with at least a baseline level of hallucinogens in his bloodstream. If you threw him in a pool completely sober, he would probably sink straight to the bottom. Right now, he's perfectly able to competently race with me.

When Ryan calls for the first time this evening, she mostly wants to find out where I am and why I've turned my tracking app off. I tell her that I'm just sitting at home with Markus and that I turned the app off because I felt under constant scrutiny, and that the point off me going away this summer – for the hundredth time – was that we would give each other some space, so that we can grow closer together again. When Ryan calls for the second time this evening, she mostly wants to find out whether I really, absolutely, most definitely didn't kiss anyone when I was out last night and that at the end of the day she doesn't mind if I did, it's just best if we're honest with each other. I tell her that I didn't, that I'm not lying, and that I completely agree with the honesty policy, and please can she trust me a little.

'God, she really must have nothing else to think about,' I tell Markus. 'I'd actually forgotten about this girl from last night. Now I'm going to call her and see what she's up to.'

'You can do what you like. I'm going to stay at my parents' tonight. In fact, what I mean is you can do what you like, but I don't really want to be around to see it. Just let her go, if you're not interested.'

I give Melanie a call, arrange to meet her out for a drink, drive Markus to his parents' house, have dinner with them, and head out to see Melanie. We go to the same tacky club where we met last night and spend a significant part of the evening making out on the dance floor, but I manage to locate the last shred of decency somewhere deep inside me and go home alone around 3am.

18

By Monday morning Markus has gone back to LA. I also haven't seen my mother around the house in the last couple of days. I'm pretty much alone. I log on to my Neon Sphere email and attempt to go through my inbox but there are too many unread messages, so I get on with some of the design work that I've been ignoring for the last few days. As this isn't very exhilarating, in fact I fear that I'm going off work altogether at the moment, I decide to email Rich and try to find out any exciting developments that might be happening in the office instead.

I write:

'Whaddup, bruh? What's good at Neon Sphere? Haven't seen you guys in ages.'

A few minutes later, Rich writes back:

'Ah, there you are. I was wondering what you're up to, how things are going, whether you still work here. It's fine though; your email address indicates to me that you do (even if nothing else does).

I won't lie to you, Parke, nothing's good at the moment. In fact, I can sum up everything that's wrong in three key updates. How do you want to hear this? Descending or ascending order?'

'Start off with the most benign development and build it up to the most mortifying one. This feeling of absolute terror that you're conveying is giving me a real kick and I would like to prolong it.'

'Good choice. Here we go then. Update 1 (low devastation levels):

VisionONE have announced – through Rothchild, of course – that "Neon Sphere's profitability is not what they would like it to be" and that they're in the "very unfortunate position" of having to "downsize" to "reflect its performance" and be able to "sustain the business moving forward". As you can see I've needed a lot of quotation marks to write this down for you. I felt that I had to stay true to VisionONE's exact message. Almost everyone has been given a two-week warning and at the end of that period a number of people will be "let go" (i.e. fired). It could be five people, it could be ten, nobody knows yet. As you can imagine, this has created a lovely working atmosphere, and everyone takes real pleasure in coming in to work every day now, even more so than before. Did you know this already? Have they given *you* warning?'

'They might have, I don't know. I haven't read my emails for over a week. I'm only a freelancer though. My only question is, how is everyone at VisionONE avoiding the fact that they can easily keep ten people, just get rid of one – Rothchild – and save themselves almost three hundred thousand dollars a year?'

'I don't know. I'm not here to answer these questions; I'm just a game designer under warning. Anyway, moving on. Update 2 (moderate devastation levels):

Despite this apparent underperformance, the severe financial strain we're under and the fact that a number of capable, somewhat hard-working people are about to lose their jobs, Rothchild has managed to demonstrate once again how many fucks he gives about this company (the number remains stable at zero) by *hiring* a brand new person. A person that he's related to. Since last week, we've had his 19-year-old nephew working full-time next to Kurt, as a "marketing executive". Whatever that is. I would like to point out that the 19-year-old, whose name is Mason, has no relevant experience or qualifications and his only discernible skill as a human being is that his mouth moves faster than his brain. On the positive side, he has now replaced his uncle as the most hated Neon Sphere member of staff. So that's something.'

'Wait, 19-year-old nephew? Are we sure this guy's not just some trick that Theo's keeping behind his wife's back?'

'That's an interesting theory. They share the same grating MinnesOHta accent, have similar vacant, cow eyes and are equally obnoxious and self-important, but I suppose none of this is conclusive.

I hope you're prepared for Update 3 (obscene devastation levels). This just happened:

As you know, Elina Pankowski's main interests are a) being wholesome and blessed and b) spreading the positivity with everyone around her. And now she's taken time off planning the most important wedding in North America this decade (hers) to organize this. First thing this morning, she went round to everyone's desk and left a print out on everyone's desk. I've scanned it and am attaching it here.'

I click on the attachment. It's a two-page A4 document in blood red Arial font that reads:

The Battle of the Cakes!!

Dear all,

We all know *summer* is here and this only means one thing: vacation time ;-) The weather is getting hotter and more and more … pleasant.
 – The last few days in the office before our summer trips are finally here – can be a bit ***tough***.
Therefore one of our young sparks (this would be you Mason ;o) has the brilliant idea of a

Summertime
Bake Off !

The event will take place on
Wednesday 13th June
The battle is currently between Mason and I and we are looking for a few more eager, enthusiastic or just nutty bakers to join us!
(Here, Elina has included a ClipArt image of a pig in a chef's hat whisking something in a bowl)
So if inside you there is this wild urge to bake than please let it out
…and surprise us with your magical
(Here, she has included a photograph of a child dressed as a wizard stirring a caldron)
Or Fairytale like
(Here she has included a photograph of a young girl dressed as a princess decorating a cookie)
… or … just creative
(Here she has included a picture of a child that I can't tell the gender of because he/she is holding a huge mixing bowl over his/her head)
baking skills!
But if you are a NON-baker – don't worry you won't miss out
As we will be in need of MANY qualified, skilled or just hungry tasters

to select the winner
(Here she has included a picture of a young girl with pigtails licking cake mixture from a spoon, right next to a picture of a baby boy laughing uproariously with chocolate all around his mouth)
All YOU will have to worry about is 'Not to pack lunch' (for at least 3 days) and find the best way
To ROLL home
(Here she has included a picture of British actor and comedian Matt Lucas dressed as Tweedledum and Tweedledee from Tim Burton's movie adaptation of *Alice in Wonderland*).
:-)
Elina

I don't respond to Rich, because I don't know what I could possibly say that won't make me sound like a homicidal psychopath and check my personal email instead. Ryan doesn't have similar concerns about sounding like a broken record, so she has written:

'Morning,

A couple of questions:

a) Have you given any thought to how long you're going to stay there this summer?
b) What kind of mood are you in at the moment? Kissing other girls or not kissing other girls?
c) Love me?

Forever yours,

Ryan'

I write back:

'Good morning, my love,

Here are your answers:

a) I don't know yet. I'm going to try and come back as early as possible though. And b) not kissing girls. Don't panic. Finally, c) absofuckinglutely.'

This reminds me that I would very much like to kiss (and possibly more) that girl from the Citizen café, Valerie, so I call her up and leave her a voicemail. Within minutes my phone rings and I get all excited for a second until I look at the number and realize that it's just somebody's calling me from the office. To make matters worse, this somebody turns out to be Theo Rothchild. Of course I already know what this is about. Rothchild starts off by asking me where I am today and I tell him that I'm working remotely from my family home in San Francisco, and I'm intending to do so for the next three months. He says that he was unaware of this, and asks me who signed off this particular arrangement. I tell him that I had a meeting with my line manager, Brett Anderson, last week and he agreed that it would be fine. I helpfully add that he can check with Brett if he wants, even though I suspect that this is no longer relevant given what he's about to tell me. He lets out a short dry cough, which comes across as an expression of both how uncomfortable this conversation is making him and how much he abhors me, and after a brief pause he breaks into a clinical, well-practiced monologue expressing his 'deep regret' about having to terminate my contract with immediate effect given Neon Sphere's current financial performance. I tell him that I understand, that it's fine, and, just to ensure that my bridges are well and truly burnt with this self-important jackass, that I hope Neon Sphere manages to come through to the other side unaffected by all the catastrophic decision-making that's been taking place over there recently. He mispronounces 'fuck you' as 'thank you' and we hang up. Oh well, it seems like I'm going to have a lot more free time than I ever expected this summer.

I exchange a few emails with people from work telling them what just happened, promise to keep in touch and even mean it, and go outside for a run. When I come back, Valerie has sent me a text. She's going away for ten days or so, but she'd love to go on a date and will give me a call when she gets back. I'm not sure I like the sound of any of this, so I don't reply. With nothing to do and no one around I wander into one of the family rooms that has never been occupied by a family and put the TV on. For reasons that I'd rather not overthink right now, I check out the Hallmark channel, only to find that it's running a quite incomprehensible 'Christmas in June' weeklong special. I start watching *Auntie Clause Is Coming To Town*, a Hallmark movie about Santa's sister relocating to Los Angeles for the month of December to drum up interest in the holiday season amongst the busy, preoccupied masses, but I turn it off halfway through. Auntie Clause is doing my head in, she's too full of Christmas spirit, I can't take it anymore. Of course it's no good focusing on the wrong part here – I did, in fact, watch half a Hallmark Christmas movie on this Monday afternoon in June, yes, I'm that lonely.

On Monday evening I get a furious phone call from Ryan, which goes a little bit like this:

'I see you've been making new friends in the Bay Area,' she says bitterly.

'What are you talking about?'

'Melanie Lindo.'

Damn. I absent-mindedly accepted this person's Facebook friend request earlier this morning.

'Yeah, what about her? She's a friend of Davis,' I met her the other night when we went out.'

'That's interesting, she's not friends with Davis on Facebook. In fact, she's only just become friends with you out of all the people I know in San Francisco.'

'You are quite the sleuth, aren't you?'

'I have to be. You'll love to hear the rest of my findings too.'

'Oh really? Go on then.'

'Melanie Lindo doesn't think that you're "the kind of person who would have a girlfriend". And that's a direct quote.'

'What the fuck, Ryan? You've been talking to her?'

'Yes, just a little bit. Why not?'

'You're embarrassing yourself, that's all.'

'I think you're creating enough embarrassment for both of us. Anyway, when I told Melanie that we've been together for over a year, she asked if we have an open relationship. Then when I picked my jaw off the keyboard and typed no, she stopped replying to me.'

'Well, that's just great. Take some random stranger's word over mine then. She must have a crush on me. That's why she friend requested me.'

'I'm sure, yes.'

'I shouldn't have accepted her. And you really shouldn't be acting like this. I really thought more of you.'

'Right. OK, well, let's leave this here for now. Just be careful. That's all.'

19

On Tuesday evening of the following week I'm talking to Markus on Skype and Markus is having several problems with his cat at the moment, including but not limited to the cat being too fluffy, too excitable, having a 'dull, not streetwise' look in his eyes like most other cats do, and being unable to pick up any tricks. He's very disappointed, he says, because he's had this vision for Frost and Frost is letting him down in every possible way.

I change the conversation to Ryan, who's been trying out different methods to force my affection. The fact that I'm not working anymore and, more to the point, that I don't seem that bothered about it reminded her, apparently, that I'm entitled and lazy and perhaps she's better off without me. That is, I'm not the one who wants to break up with her; she's the one who wants to break up with me. That suits me very fine, so in the forty-eight hours that this new approach lasted, I kinda sat back and let things unfold in a casual, offhand way, which only resulted in her going in a spin and abruptly backtracking. I'm now copying her latest email to Markus:

'Listen, I don't want you to think that I've made any decision or anything has changed while you've been away. I've mentioned this before aaaaaaaaages ago, but I'm adaptable and get used to situations. I'm almost used to living alone again now, but that doesn't mean that I'm not looking forward to you coming back or that I don't want to be your girlfriend. When you're back hopefully we can have a fresh start and go from there x.'

'I'm really not here to encourage whatever it is that you're doing with this woman, but it really doesn't seem that she's adapted and got used to any situations to me,' Markus says.

'I imagine not. But why do you say that?'

'Well, she's still coming round here all the time. Sometimes alone, sometimes with that friend of hers.'

'Reed?'

'Yeah, maybe. She came over on Sunday and brought me homemade cookies.'

'What?'

'Yes, homemade cookies. They were very nice, actually.'

'You ate them?'

'Of course I ate them. It was late at night and I was stoned.'

'I'd be careful, if I were you.'

'Why? I'm not the one treating her like a dick. She has no reason to kill me.'

'She might just kill you to get to me.'

'Not for the first time, you're suffering from delusions of grandeur. Like, people are scheming and plotting and organizing murder just to get back to you. Who are you?'

He takes a pause to light up his bong.

'Can I tell you more about the cookies now?'

'No.'

'They were double dark chocolate and pomegranate ones.'

'That's not even a thing I recognize. I wonder where she learnt how to make those. Doesn't sound like something they would be having in Albuquerque.'

'I don't know. But I want more. I might go and buy some pomegranates or something.'

'Yes, then give Ryan a call and she'll come over and bake for you.'

He drops his jaw and widens his eyes, as if this were some ingenious idea that he's definitely going to put in practice. I'm beginning to lose him.

'Let me look up pomegranates on Wikipedia.'

'Can I go before you do that?'

'No, stay. You don't have anything else to do, do you?'

I don't answer that and he continues.

'OK, pomegranates are like some magical fruit or something. I really want to get some. Did you know that they've been used for centuries to dye things naturally?'

'That's fascinating', I say.

'Yes. People use them to dye fabric, Easter eggs, hair...'

'What people are those?'

'You know... people. People of bygone eras.'

I'm really starting to worry about Markus. I think the brain damage is becoming more acute. Does he only exist to remind us that seemingly having it all doesn't guarantee happiness? Is he just a walking life lesson in the form of a human being that will inevitably implode, leaving everyone around him with a feeling of immense guilt because we didn't step in when we could?

'Perhaps you should try to dye your cat. Then, once that's been successful, you can create a whole new series of products for Ryan, as a reward for the baked goods she'll been providing. You can create clothes dye, make up, highlights for her hair. All in the same shade of dirty brown/red. Eventually, you can start your own business, of course.'

'This is fantastic. Can you please write it down and send it to me in an email? I'll put it straight into my "Latest Business Ventures" Gmail folder. In fact, I'll probably try to open a new Gmail small business account. What do you think of MarkusWillDyeForYou@gmail.com? You know, "Dye" spelt dee why ee.'

'That's pretty good, but you probably need something with a bit of a pun, a double entendre. What you've chosen has a singular meaning, it's not very interesting.'

He looks at me lost, with his red sleepy eyes and says, 'I'd dye everyday if I could'. This cracks him up. He starts laughing maniacally, takes another hit, and we hang up.

I'm not ready to sleep yet, so I take my laptop and go downstairs to get myself a soda and sit on the patio. It's now past midnight. This is a very risky move given the high probability that I'm going to come across my mother, who has usually built up a pretty good buzz by this hour and feels confident enough to wander outside her bedroom. I go to the kitchen, pick up a drink and walk towards the outside patio, and for a moment there I think that I'm safe, as I'm not faced with the smell of tobacco that traditionally gives away her presence. It turns out that she's tricked me and is sitting there on the swing just drinking. I feel as sorry for her as I do annoyed. I probably should just turn around and go back to my room, but I guess I'm feeling totally reckless, so I take a seat at the table and start playing *Civilization* instead. She actually takes a few minutes to register that I'm there.

'What are you doing, sweetie?' she slurs.

'Playing a game.'

It takes her the best part of the next half hour to process this, during which I've built a small city, but eventually she responds:

'You're very bright.'

So much time has passed that I don't even know whether this is part of the same conversation anymore. Am I very bright because I'm playing a game? Or am I very bright overall, independent of my current activity? This is the slowest dialogue I've ever participated in and I'm not sure whether the usual rules apply. It's so easy to get lost.

Another very long pause follows and I'm starting to think that she's fallen asleep – I dare not look in her direction for fear of actually catching her eye and being dragged into a faster, still nonsensical conversation – until she finally adds:

'Your father was also very bright.'

I really would like to be able to follow her thought process during these times. I'd love for somebody to develop a computer program that tracks and interprets all the little electrochemical signals that are transmitted between the nerve cells that make up her brain. I want to follow these signals one by one and see how the external stimulus of me playing *Civilization* leads to evaluating my intellect, then leads to her forgotten partner from a quarter of a century ago. I want this computer program to also factor in decades of alcohol and pharmaceutical abuse and I want it to be able to present an alternate thought chain, had this particular subject not gang-raped her nervous system for the majority of her lifetime. Perhaps this is something I'll develop this summer. Perhaps I'll just spend the summer playing *Civilization*.

'Yes, he was *very* bright. He was also very dark.'

Oh good, she's still with us. What the hell is she talking about?

'Can you say that about somebody? He was very bright and very dark. There, I've said it,' she continues.

Her words must sound like an intellectual conundrum to her right now. Don't think that I'm missing the irony of both my mother and my best friend seemingly occupying a constant zombie state of detachment and self-amusement, unable to fully connect with their surroundings.

Mom lights a cigarette and calls out my name. 'Are you listening to me?' she asks. I decide that the best way to avoid participating in this is to reply 'yes' and continue staring at my screen.

Unsatisfied, she gets up and starts pacing on the patio. Within seconds, she walks up behind me and puts her hands on my shoulders. I can feel the heat of the cigarette near my left ear. I tilt forward slightly, attempting to make her move her hands, but she keeps hold of me and leans over to place a kiss on the right side of my neck. I stand up abruptly, causing her to stumble backwards and drop her cigarette. I pick it up for her, put my laptop under my arm, and go back in the house with a snappy 'goodnight'.

20

On Thursday morning when I wake up, I see the following email from Ryan:

'Missing me?'

I write back:

'I miss you when I wake up and have coffee.

I miss you when I go for lunch.

I miss you when I'm with my family.

I miss you most when I go to bed.

So yeah, I miss you.'

I receive her reply fewer than ten seconds later, which makes me think that either she had this written already and was waiting for me to get back to her first message, or she can type really, really fast and at least Boston University is good for something:

'Good, I miss you too. I want things to work out between us. I'm a little sad now about everything that's happened and I hope that everything that's happened isn't substantial enough to put an end to us. I need you in my life.'

I feel obliged to write something similar back. I don't know, maybe I'm thinking that on some level I can see myself with her again at some point. I'm thinking that maybe I don't want to burn this bridge just yet. There's no chance in hell that I want to go back there right now and be around her, but who knows how I'll feel in a few weeks' time?

I type 'I want that too' and send it off.

On Saturday I have an afternoon date in the city with Valerie, whose mysterious ten days away wasn't just an excuse never to meet up after all. This is something I prepare for by spending Thursday and Friday sunbathing and occasionally doing laps in the outdoor swimming pool. I'm not convinced that all this exercise and tanning will be worth it, as an afternoon date in Golden Gate park doesn't sound very promising to me sexually and I might end up having to keep my clothes on, but I'm going to go anyway and see what happens.

My first impression when I see her this time, making it my second impression overall, is that she looks even better than I remembered. This might have something to do with the fact that she's not wearing a stupid waitress apron, something that usually tends to ruin people's looks. My subsequent thought following my first impression is that I really want to sleep with this kid. She's got this thing going where her upper arms are as long and almost as thin as her forearms and, similarly, her thighs are as long and only a little bit bigger than her calves. That's my favorite physical attribute a girl can have. In actual fact, aesthetically, she reminds me of Ryan. Personality-wise she seems about four hundred times more laid back. In biological terms, this is the perfect combination.

We walk all the way across to Stow Lake and sit down on the grass by the boathouse. She keeps commenting how nice this is. I keep thinking the same. She says that she doesn't work at the restaurant anymore; she gave up the job the day after we met. Neither of us has any real plans for this summer. It's pretty damn cool talking to a girl who doesn't think this makes me some huge layabout loser right away. She's at least giving me a chance and can go on to discover how much of a layabout loser I am a bit later on. When I put my hand on her leg to brush off a tiny bug that I may or may not have actually been there, she doesn't flinch. When I move closer to see the freckles on her nose that she's complaining about, she pulls me towards herself and kisses me on the lips. There's a slight sting from the raspberry flavored lip balm she's been applying over the last half hour, since we sat down here. For some reason, it's making me like her more. It's like there's a small electric charge between us, like this tingle is caused by some extraordinary connection that she and I happen to have, instead of whatever chemicals are currently covering her lips. I want to ask her what she's doing for the rest of the day, I want to invite her back to my place, but I don't want to scare her away by being too hasty. Thankfully, she does it for me.

'It's so hot sitting here,' she says. 'A boy like you must have a pool at his house. Right?'

She's very perceptive. I wonder what gave it away.

'What? Why would you think that?' I ask.

'So you don't?'

'Actually, yes.'
'Let's go.'

Back in Hillsborough, I take her around to the pool and go upstairs to get changed and pretend that I'm looking for a swimsuit for her to wear. It's obvious that there's nothing like that just casually lying around the house, because, well, why would there be? I'm sure whatever discarded items from teenage girls I brought over when I last lived here have been disposed of a long time ago. I put on a pair of gym shorts over my boxer shorts, because if she can't go in the water then surely neither can I, and head back downstairs. On the way there I pass Denning, who tells me that he's taken towels and drinks outside for my guest and me. His face when he says this is completely expressionless and non-judgmental, clearly indicating that something really worth judging is taking place out there. I now fully expect to step out and find this person doing naked backflips into the pool. As it happens, she's just swimming in her underwear. I decide that it might not be such a bad idea to join in on this free-spirited approach. I take a sip of whatever this juice is that Denning has brought out as a last minute attempt to act cool by delaying my physical attack on of her, and proceed to dive in in gym shorts, boxer shorts, Wayfarers and all.

We start splashing water, chasing, and grabbing each other underwater, as I believe is compulsory in hydro-specific amorous situations. To my shock, disbelief and instant arousal, within minutes she takes it to the next level of soft-core porn movie clichés by removing her panties and throwing them over my head onto the poolside. This is the exact moment when our long-term prospects suddenly die, not that I was exactly looking for long-term prospects with a former waitress of completely unidentified credentials and two nipple piercings. Very, very soon after that I climb out of the pool, grab the towels and take this upstairs to my bedroom. Valerie has the audacity to mock the décor ("Four poster bed? Seriously? Who are you?) and from the little I know of her, this seems to be completely in character. Of course, I take this criticism as seriously as I would take any criticism from a person who's strutting around a stranger's house dripping wet, wearing only a soaked bra and a white towel in the middle of a Saturday afternoon.

When everything is done and Valerie's in the shower, I answer a FaceTime call from Markus, whose genius idea this time is to place his cell phone in front of Frost instead, in an attempt to make me think that the cat is calling me. The surprises don't end there though, as the second face I see on my phone screen is also unexpected: Ryan beaming a smile from Markus' living room. This sends some very abrupt shock waves down the length my spine and, having fixed what I can only guess appears as an uncomfortable grin on my lips to make up for the terror in my eyes, I dart outside my room and down the corridor.

'Surprise!' she yells.

'Hahahahahaha', I laugh maniacally. 'My favorite people in the world hanging out together?'

'Ha, yes. I came over to say hi to Frost.'

'That's sweet. I miss you guys.'

'We miss you too.'

'I'm lonely without you and I really can't wait to get back to LA. Listen, I've got to go now though. I was just heading out with mom.'

Her mood instantly turns. 'She goes out of the house now?'

I decide to keep playing stupid. Smiling, I say:

'Well, sometimes. I wanted to take her for a drive. Maybe get some dinner or something.'

'Well, OK. You and your mom have fun then.'

She hangs up before I get the chance to say goodbye and I walk back to my room where I find Valerie sitting naked on the white armchair. I go down on my knees, put her legs over my shoulders and start eating her out.

21

On Monday of the following week, like any other day of any other week, I don't have much to do apart from surf the internet, play video games and email people. I'm coming to realize that, first of all, I don't have that many friends in San Francisco anymore and, second of all, Los Angeles is a much better city for acquaintances who have no job – or have a very vague and unidentified job anyway – and are available to socialize at any time on week days. Thinking of Markus, I give him a call. This is a safe time to talk to him, as surely Ryan has to go to work sometimes and he's likely to be alone.

It's just after noon and he's currently in the long, arduous process of waking up. The first thing he says to me is this:

'Did you know that cats didn't meow in their natural, wild environment and they only developed this vocal expression to mimic human voices after the were domesticated?'

'Well they're not doing a very good job then, are they? Call me when you're awake and ready to talk about anything other than cats.'

I then think to email someone at Neon Sphere just to see what's going on over there. I write to Kurt:

'Hello. How's everything?'

Kurt takes no longer than ten minutes to write back:

'Everyhung (I'm not exactly sure how to interpret this misspelling but I'll keep it and think about it) is as it should be I guess. Here's a summary of work-related news:

a) Charlotte Ryland looks really good today, probably needs to wash her hair though for a perfect score.

b) Elina Pankowski's Summer Bake Off, originally due to happen last Wednesday, was cancelled due to a complete lack of interest. Hoping the same will apply to her wedding.

c) I haven't seen Kwasi in reception for a few days. Consequently, I'm assuming that he now has a new job selling weed or handguns or both in West Compton.

d) Mason Rothchild, the loathsome 19-year-old that Theo inexplicably brought in and gave a job to, only lasted a couple of weeks. He's now gone. Initially it was a permanent, full-time position, but it is suspected that the public uproar led to his early demise. He sent a laughable group email out before he left. I'm copying it below.

"Hi Guys,

As you know today I am leaving Neon Sphere after having a fantastic two weeks here, I have learned so much in such a short period of time and I am extremely thankful to everyone who has taken their time to look after me and teach me all I have learned. It has been an amazing opportunity, which has really opened my eyes to the ways of the world. I wish everyone the best of luck in the future.

It has truly been a pleasure,

Mason"

You're welcome.'
I write back:
'c) You're forgetting that almost odds-on possibility that Kwasi has simply been deported.
d) Was it you who opened Mason's eyes to the way of the world?'
Kurt replies:
'd) Yes, before I came into his life, he was just a mouthy, over-confident teen with the brain capacity of a baseball sock and the life experience of an indoor kitten. Oh wait...'
I'm kinda done with this and my next move is to kill a few hours on Facebook. I try to find Valerie, but I don't actually know her last name yet and after going through a few dozen Valeries based in San Francisco I give up and take a look at Ryan's profile. Her latest update is offering congratulations to Rae Prinz and Tommy Gillman for setting a date for their wedding in September. Isn't it funny how she wants to be friends with all of my friends that she normally hates now that I'm away? When I get bored, I go to the family room and have lunch whilst

watching a Hallmark film double feature celebrating Hallmark channel's Summertime Madness week, before falling asleep.

I'm woken up from my nap halfway through Candy Cotton Beach, a coming-of-age teen drama about a group of friends who find love, laughter and themselves in the pretentious Orange County beach club they've spent their summer working at, by a phone call from Ryan.

'What are you doing?' she asks.

'Just taking a nap.'

'In the middle of the day?'

'I can't nap at night. I'm asleep then.'

'I see. So do you intend to do anything else this summer? Maybe get another job or something? Go anywhere?'

She sounds really worked up. Needs to chill the fuck out, as far as I'm concerned. Don't know what brought this on, but there's usually no reason anyway. She just sits there gritting her teeth and attempting to put up with situations she's not comfortable with, until finally something snaps. This goes in cycles.

'Um, I don't really know. I told you, I'm here to have some time to myself.'

'That's a hell of a lot of time. What do you do all day? I'd be bored out of my mind without a job.'

'Well they let me go, there wasn't anything I could do.'

'Why don't you try to find a new one?'

'I'm planning to. Lighten up.'

'And how do you suggest I do that?'

I don't know what to say, so I don't say anything. We stay on the phone in complete silence for several seconds, until she finally tells me that she has to get back to work and hangs up. Thankfully none of this has managed to unsettle me in any effective way, and I fall back asleep soon after.

When I wake up a couple of hours later, I check my iPad and have emails from Markus and Ryan. I read Markus' first:

'Yeah hi, I know that you'll think I'm joking, but I really, genuinely received this email below. The sender's address is thehollywoodsexclub@gmail.com and they said:

"Secret Bondage Sex Invitation

A friend or acquaintance has suggested we contact you as they indicate your preference might be for secret completely anonymous sexual encounters with similar men and women. All our women are educated, attractive, slim and voluptuous. All our men are professional, muscular, white and hung. The person recommending you has indicated you are suitable in terms of body and sexual preference for our group. This group of individuals has been meeting for the last 5 years in Hollywood with great success. We do not wish to know your name or anything about you. We will not reveal who recommended you or reveal any communication of yours to them. The meeting involves the use of masks and leather equipment and gear and is a totally safe and sexy environment. If you reply to this email you will be further instructed."

I write back:
'Personally, I think you should do it. It sounds like a nice, enjoyable activity that will get you socializing with similar-minded people and, you heard them, it's totally safe. It's worth asking a few questions first, mind you:
What is the minimum level of education that the women have achieved?
Why are all the men white?
Do you need to bring your own mask and leather equipment or will this be provided?
Why did they not contact me?
Etc.
Once they've given satisfactory answers to the points above, you can go.'
I send this off and go on to read the email I've received from Ryan. Ryan has written:
'I think you should totally not get another job ever, seems a bit pointless, no? Stay there and do nothing.'
I see that she's online on Skype – she must still be at work – and type a chat message:

'Saw your email. You're right. I should just catch the first flight to LA and start frenziedly applying for jobs instead of spending the next few weeks here like I was planning to. It's one or the other, right?'

She's there and writes back:

'It's mainly the frame of mind that goes with sitting there doing nothing that concerns me. It's the frame of mind that's led you your whole life.'

'I'm sick of having to defend myself against your ever-present fear that I'll never achieve anything. I achieved enough before you were even around.'

'You're the kind of guy who leaves everything up to chance and is certain that things will work out for you every time, but you only remember the times that they did, so you've got a sense of achievement.'

'Why do you have to be so bitter? Some things just happen to fall on my lap. What do you want me to do? Disown my family and take a pitiful little job somewhere and get paid next to nothing while I "work my way up?"'

'Happy as I am that you don't have to do this, I will never, ever be proud that my (almost) 25-year-old boyfriend's only source of accomplishment is his background. And the "falling on your lap" thing is everything that's unattractive about your personality. Nothing falls on anyone's lap ever. Anything good that happens comes with a price. And the price here is your low self-esteem. This is caused by having the misguided belief that things will "fall on your lap" forever. They never did and they never will. You are human.'

'I don't even know what to say about the low self-esteem comment. Can we fucking stop arguing already? This sucks.'

I send the last sentence and immediately log off. This is driving me insane. It feels like all my blood is rushing to the top of my head and I'm getting a throbbing headache, pounding to the beat of my heart. I get up, walk to the window and open it and close it four times. I repeat this pattern four times in total. That's four fours. I can see the pool from here and I decide that a better activity would be to go down there and swim laps in intervals of four. Four laps of front crawl, then breaststroke, then backstroke, and then butterfly. This will conceal my obsessive compulsiveness behind an actual activity, hopefully masking the disorder.

When I'm done I go back upstairs, shower and get changed. I check my messages for the first time since I turned off my iPad a while ago and only find a new email from Markus. Ryan hasn't written. She hasn't called, hasn't texted, nothing. I try to forget about this for now and call Davis up. We meet up for dinner in the city and then I go back home and have an early night.

I wake up at 10. Ryan has now written. I was wondering how long it would take for her to apologize. Her message says:

'Parke, this is a very difficult email to write. I almost don't want to write this or even finish the thought in my head, but I think it's for the best if we take an actual break. A proper separation. I don't want to make big public announcements, but I think what we're doing at the moment isn't working and we have to acknowledge it. So I suggest that we're actual completely out of this relationship, for as long as you're away anyway. When you come back, we can meet up face to face and discuss and see what we think. I certainly am not doing this because I want to be single or because I want to meet other people (even though until we discuss this face to face we will be single and you can do whatever you want though I'd rather not hear / know about it please). I'm doing it because I don't think I want to be your girlfriend right now.

I see a lack of drive and motivation in you that I have absolutely no respect for. And I think it's not right to be in a relationship with somebody that you don't respect.

Perhaps this is an unfair assessment. However, I'm so angry with the life choices that you've made and keep making and the general idleness, that even if I'm wrong I still don't think I should be in a relationship with you. There must be somebody out there who loves you for exactly the person that you are and doesn't see you as this unmotivated person. I love you too, but the perception that I have of you annoys the hell out of me. Please don't get angry. I completely acknowledge that this is my perception of it and I might be completely wrong. But I just can't do this anymore if I think like that.

So that's that. I still want you to come back soon and I look forward to seeing you. And I still want to be your friend and I want to go to Tommy and Rae's wedding in September with you, etc. I also don't want to break our link on Facebook and get people talking. But I don't want to be your girlfriend. Until we discuss this face to face.

I'm really upset that this hasn't worked out. I think we both really wanted it to.'

I read her message again concentrating on every word, even the ones where she's repeating herself, driving her point home. If this is the out I thought that I wanted, why does it feel like I've just been kicked to the ground?

22

Ryan's decision to dump me and my subsequent bad mood only last for a day and a half. I swear to God, some girls have no idea how to play their game. After not contacting each other for about thirty-four hours, she sends me a text on Tuesday afternoon that says:

'The plant that you gave me at the end of last year has been going yellow. After looking this up online, I realize I may have been over-watering it.'

She ends this transmission with a sad face.

My question is two-fold: when did I give her a plant and why is she telling me this? Regardless, I decide that the best way to regain control of this relationship and stop feeling bad about myself is to play along, and I reply:

'I love you.'

She texts right back:

'Once again in my life I'm doing the right thing, but perhaps too much of it.'

I write back just repeating the sad face she sent me one text message ago as an empathetic yet non-committal response and she immediately calls me up. She's been very sad since we broke up, she says, and she thinks she was too hasty. In fact, breaking up with me wasn't just hasty – it was stupid. She's happy to give me space to sort myself out and she doesn't care whether I work or what I do with my life. She just wants to be with me.

Ambushed by this peculiar change of direction I don't feel like I have any choice but to say yes, and I agree to be part once again of this ambiguous passive-aggressive hurtful entanglement that we call our relationship. I do add, however, that I really want to see her put into practice the things that she just said and actually demonstrate her acceptance instead of just talking about it. Also, moving forward I want her to give me some proper space, because in the past few weeks that I've been in San Francisco, I've felt like she's been trying to track down my every move and control my life remotely, which isn't conducive to me missing her and wanting to be with her.

I must have not given her credit enough intellectually, because she immediately catches my drift and asks whether this means that I want to sleep with other people. I say yes. She's broken enough to accept this. We wrap this up by telling each other how happy we are that we've worked things out again and hang up.

I don't even put the phone down before texting Valerie to ask what she's doing tonight. I go downstairs to find something to eat leaving my phone in my room so that I'm surprised to find a reply when I come back, but it's from Ryan instead who's got in touch to ask:

'Do you miss me yet?'

I write back:

'Yeah, definitely. You?'

She says 'Aha' and I go out for a run, leaving my phone in my room again. Valerie doesn't text back until 2am that night (I see it when I wake up in the morning) but at least she's free this evening and we arrange for her to come over.

She stays overnight and we end up spending most of the next day together as well, but then she has to go away on one of her mysterious trips again, this time for a week. I'm not at all curious where those trips are or what she does there and, to be honest, I find it more of a relief than anything else that she's not around all the time. Despite my lack of interest, she's simply dying to share and just before she drives off on Thursday evening, I have to sit there and listen to the shocking revelation that every now and then she and a friend go up to Humbolt County and get paid $2,500 a week for trimming illegal marijuana plants. This is shocking, of course, only in the way that it's so utterly predictable and banal. A real shock would have been to reveal a moneymaking activity that doesn't involve drugs, perhaps prostitution of some description, something that doesn't require a complete lack of morals anyway, but nonetheless, I react in the way I expect that she wants me to, with 'Oh my God', 'Are you serious', 'That's pretty cool', etc. She leaves and promises to be back on the following Friday, not that anyone asked her to make any promises, not that anyone will care if she doesn't keep them.

The following Friday is actually a day to look forward to regardless of Valerie's return, as it's the Fourth of July and one can hope that it will provide a welcome distraction in what's turning out to be a very slow summer. For one thing, Markus flies in at the weekend with the intention to spend the whole week here and attend his parents' party on the 4th.

The Brandts have a long-standing tradition of throwing this now famous, lavish Independence Day party at their mansion. I must have spent every single Fourth of July when I was growing up there, which has been very convenient seeing that nobody at my house was keen to celebrate any holidays (my mother doesn't operate on a conventional calendar). Nowadays the party mainly serves a purpose for the Brandts to show off their Nazi money and reinforce their social status in the Bay Area. I believe that initially, when Markus' great grandfather started it back in the 1940s soon after relocating here from Europe, its poorly concealed intention was to ingratiate the family with the locals, who understandably must have been suspicious and possibly quite hostile towards this German family turning up out of nowhere and appropriating much of the area using their vast, inexplicable wealth. And an annual party of Gatsby-esque proportions on the nation's most treasured holiday was the quickest and easiest way to generate goodwill and change people's perceptions.

For me, the most amusing thing about all this is that Markus will inevitably have to take on this tradition at some point, being the only male heir in the family, and it's just absurd to even consider that Markus will ever have developed the sense of skill or responsibility to pull something like this off. It's ironic how boundless wealth has the tendency to turn its proprietors completely incapable of sustaining it. The only way he could eventually front the Brandt family brand would be by simply being a carefully regulated puppet, whose only input would be the provision of his physical image.

On Friday I wake up quite late, just after 11.30am, and have breakfast in bed whilst checking messages and online posts. Everyone appears to be very excited about the holiday, save for Ryan who's stuck in LA with no specific plans. We went to the Brandt party together last year and she finds the thought of me being here without her this year after all that's happened between us (and I quote from her morning email) "really heartbreaking". Judging by Facebook, she's going to be particularly lonely today, as a lot of the people we know in LA seem to have gone home for long weekends, seeing that the 4th falls on a Friday this year. In fact, it's nice to see several Facebook friends post family pictures this Fourth of July. It's often easy to forget that some of these guys actually came from people.

As soon as I've finished eating and taken a shower, I pick up my clothes for the evening and drive over to the Brandts'. Markus is still in his bedroom half asleep, playing some unlistenable noise on his stereo. I fail to understand how somebody can lie in bed and relax while this racket is on. It sounds like a defective steam train going through a tunnel, with an added ascending intensity. Even the cat – which he's brought with him – is cowering in the center of the room as far away as possible from the four surrounding speakers placed in each corner, looking completely traumatized. This is not an unexpected state of mind for anyone who's unfortunate enough to be Markus' roommate, whether human or pet.

'Is this your set for later? I can't wait to hear it at the main party,' I say.

'Yes, I think it will go down well, right?'

'Your cat begs to differ. I'm going to let him out, he doesn't seem to be enjoying this very much.'

'No!'

He jumps out of bed in terror.

'The dogs keep chasing him. I shouldn't have brought him here in the first place.'

'Oh well, I'm sure he won't be any more uncomfortable than the date that I'm bringing.'

'Oh yes. The now unemployed former waitress.'

'And marijuana plant horticulturist, don't forget.'

'Don't try to build her up. She only just trims them. I'm looking forward to seeing how she interprets the Summer Black Tie dress code anyway.'

This reminds me to text Valerie and tell her there's a Summer Black Tie dress code, and then Markus and I take his little sister to the park to get her out of everyone's way.

23

Fireworks at the Brandts' Fourth of July party go off at 9.46pm sharp, in order to eclipse the Foster City display that takes place between 9.30pm and 9.45pm just a few miles down the road. Year after year, Foster City really has no chance. Not long after the fireworks are done, Markus, Davis, Davis' date, Valerie and I leave the main party and go back in the house, where those guys can freely smoke and inhale whatever substances they feel like, less discreetly. We're upstairs on the first floor balcony facing the grounds at the back of the house. I've spoken to Ryan at very regular intervals through the whole evening, even being on the phone to her when the fireworks were going off, so as to make her feel like she was part of this.

Markus passes a joint around and they all take a few drags. This isn't very much fun at all for me. I put my arm around Valerie's waist, lean into her and ask her to come with me. As we're walking inside the house Ryan calls me again, but this time I ignore it. I take Valerie to the guest bedroom where I'm staying and start undressing her. The whole thing takes maybe twenty minutes, we don't even have sex or anything, but in that time Ryan has called five or six times. So much for giving me space.

I return her calls when Valerie and I are back on the balcony with the others.

'Where have you been?' she asks.

'I'm still here at the party.'

'But why haven't you been answering your phone?'

'I left it in the other room charging. We're back in the house now.'

'Are you sure?'

'Of course I'm sure.'

'I know that you're lying.'

I stay quiet.

'You don't have to lie. You can do whatever you want.'

'OK.'

'Were you with a girl?'

'No.'

She doesn't say anything. The silence makes me think that she's about to cry or something.

'Fine then,' I say and walk back in the house. 'Yes, I was.'

'Who was it?'

'Some girl here. You don't know her.'

'What did you do?'

'We just fooled around.'

'Did you have sex?'

'No. You need to calm down. I was out of your reach for, like, fifteen minutes.'

'What does she look like? Did she go down on you?'

'Oh my God. Why do you want details? Can't we just leave it? You seem to be very upset. And I did nothing wrong.'

'I'm not upset. I know we agreed it's fine to do this. I just didn't expect you to go rushing into it.'

'I didn't rush into anything. It just happened.'

'Does this girl know that you have a girlfriend back home anyway?'

'I think she does. I've been telling everyone here that we're still together, and that I can't wait to see you when I get back to LA.'

'I see. I have to go now.'

I start telling her not to be upset, but she's already hung up. I walk back out and join the others. Markus asks if that was Ryan and I nod yes. Valerie asks who Ryan is and I say that she's 'some girl I was seeing back in LA.' To her credit, Valerie doesn't seem disturbed or curious by this in the slightest. Sometimes it pays off to socialize with amoral hippies.

Still, I'm kinda bummed by the whole incident and I don't want to hang around for much longer. I tell Markus that I'm going to call it a night and start walking back to my room. Valerie says that she'll be there shortly.

Minutes later, I get yet another call from Ryan.

'Is she going to spend the night there?'

'Probably. Everyone's been drinking, she can't drive home.'

'Can't Markus' driver or your driver take her home?'

'Ryan, that's ridiculous. Please don't worry about it. Nothing's going to happen. We're just going to sleep.'

'That's even worse. You're my boyfriend. Making out with some random girl is one thing, but spending the night together and sharing a bed? What are you trying to do?'

'I'm not trying to do anything. I'm sorry.'

She hangs up on me again and I turn mine off.

When I wake up in the morning, Valerie is lying next to me still sleeping. I decide to get my stuff together and leave as quickly as possible. The house is so busy with people clearing up from last night, and I just want to get in my car and drive home.

I turn my phone on for the first time whilst having breakfast in the sunroom next to the indoor swimming pool back at my house. I try to guess the number of messages Ryan will have left, but it's early morning, I'm still groggy and I can't count that high. Surprisingly, there's only one email and one voicemail. The email, sent at 1.20am, reads:

'I would still like to know how the whole thing happened if "you were telling everyone that we are still together".

1) By kissing you, did this girl think that you were cheating on me?
2) Or had you told her that "we're on a break, and it's OK to kiss"?
3) Or perhaps that we are together but have an open relationship?

I would be interested to hear the answer to that, if you could please tell me.'

I get a sudden urge to launch myself to the bottom of the pool headfirst just to get out of this progressively unbearable situation, but I must loathe myself even more than I already thought, as I proceed undeterred to listen to her voicemail instead. This was left around 7am this morning. The tone she strives for is 'bold' and 'in control'. The tone that I perceive is 'powerless' and 'desperate'.

She says that she's thought about it and that she can't have this anymore. We've decided to be together, haven't we, and we shouldn't be allowed to fool around with other people. I can stay here as long as I want, but this is the right time to try to be responsible and act like a grown up for once in my life – our relationship will have to be monogamous and that's that.

Well, that's one thing we agree on. That really is that. I'm now ready to tell her directly what I've been avoiding over the last two months. I call her up and just say that I don't want to be with her anymore. It's not that I want to have a break, it's not that I need some distance, it's not that I need time to clear my head. I just don't want to be her boyfriend. She lets out a scream and starts sobbing. This makes me feel approximately nothing. Struggling through her crying, she begs me to change my mind. I say no. This is excruciating. She's now properly hysterical, screaming out, 'why are you doing this to me?' over and over again. Once that's done, she pleads with me to feel sorry for her. Not paraphrasing or anything, just directly stating 'Please feel sorry for me'. It's odd. I tell her that I'm going to end this conversation unless she calms herself down immediately. As a response, she informs me screaming that she's on the floor crying (I can attest to the latter, if not to her actual position in the room).

The whole thing goes on for about half an hour, even though I would actually believe anyone who tells me that I've just lost a decade on this phone call. Finally comprehending that I'm not going to change my mind as a consequence of her frenzy, she lets me go. I tell her to go over to my place, let herself into Markus' and take some Valium or something.

'I still love you so much,' she says.

'You know what, I still love you too.'

'I actually believe that. But I also believe that you'll never love anyone as much as you hate yourself,' she says, and I manage to hang up on her fragments of a second before she has the chance to do the same to me.

24

The thing about Valerie is that she lives on a boat. This is not some small towable houseboat with one tiny room that serves as living area, kitchen, and bedroom with pull down bunk bed all at the same time. This is a large, late 19th century houseboat that has three kitchens and sleeps up to fifteen people across three decks. She's one of four or five people who permanently stay there as part of a very peculiar, kind of communal living arrangement. It's a very cool houseboat but strange set up, the exact details of which remain unclear to me still. Of course she doesn't pay any rent.

Valerie met the owner of the boat, an older guy named Saul, while at a garage sale looking at a surfboard. He basically invited her there and then to come live on his boat for free. I don't know whom to think less of in that scenario. The older guy who hastily invites the young girl to come live at his place, or the young girl who readily accepts? Saul is hardly ever around, anyway, and has a very dubious professional background. Something about running a few web companies at some point in the past, whatever that means. I've spent a lot of my time in Sausalito on the boat in the three weeks since I broke up with Ryan and I've not seen him once. I've seen a lot of Valerie's roommates though – both the permanent ones and the rotating cast of people who drop in and out for a few hours or days at a time. All of them young, earthy, seemingly with a lot of free time in their hands.

On some level I want this to be some creepy sexual thing. That is, I want all these people to be staying there in exchange for weird sexual favors. That would make a lot of sense. Unfortunately this doesn't seem to be the case. If Saul keeps all those people there to fuck them, why does he never come over to do so? And, not that this necessarily proves anything (after all, why couldn't these sex slaves be allowed to have their own romantic lives outside their duties?) but two of the other permanent boat residents are a couple and everyone else seems to be actively and openly dating outsiders.

The fact that I'm dating Valerie, of course, hasn't escaped Ryan. She sent a very long email last week to tell me so and I even read most of it:

'Parke,

I think things have reached a stage, which is completely heartbreaking for me. Over the last couple of months we've had so many ups and downs and so many discussions and conversations that have gone several different ways. I think what the gist for me, however, is that you have not taken anything on board about my feelings or what I think. And I know that we're not together right now, but even so, your behavior continues to be nothing short of humiliating for me.

Even now that you're single, I expect a little bit of mutual understanding between us, i.e. some discretion on both of our parts, so we don't make each other seem like a fool publicly to all our friends and acquaintances. In our conversations you promised me that you were being discreet and that it would all be fine.

However, evidence has shown me that you are unable to follow any of the agreements we've made and have shown zero interest or ability to try to adapt your behavior even slightly for things to work between us. Please see below a conversation I had with a guy called Kai Hubbard. I saw that you became friends on Facebook recently and looked at his profile, where I saw pictures of you hanging out on some boat with all of those fucked up kids. A couple of days ago he messaged me for the first time unprompted (I didn't message anyone asking for stories, HE did) and you can see the rest. These messages were sent while you were living on that boat with them, apparently.

Kai Hubbard
"Hi Ryan,
Your profile says you live in Los Angeles. Have I seen you in San Francisco? Kai"

Ryan Dalton
"Hi Kai,
Yeah I live in LA, though my boyfriend is from San Francisco and I've

been there a few times over the last year. I can't remember whether we've actually met, though you look familiar."

Kai Hubbard
"Cool – let me know when you're back in SF!"

Ryan Dalton
"Will do! Think I'll be there soon."

Kai Hubbard
"Do I know your boyfriend? Is he still in SF or does he live in LA with you?"

Ryan Dalton
"He's moved to LA but he's been in San Francisco for the last month or so. His name is Parke Hudson. Just seen that you're friends here..."

Kai Hubbard
"Haha, I know Parke. He's your boyfriend?! Are you guys in an open relationship?"

Kai Hubbard
"Sorry, didn't mean to be too personal with that question. I just would have never thought Parke had a "girlfriend""

If you remove yourself from the situation and see this objectively, you'll see how offensive and ridiculous it is. It's one thing to be taking a break from someone (as we are) and be having fun with other people, but to do it in a manner that's so blatant, so public and so open that invites people to appear completely incredulous at the suggestion that you might have had any commitment to anyone in the recent past (to the point where they use the word girlfriend in quotation marks as if they don't believe me for bringing it up as a possibility) is just, well, a cunty thing to do. I mean, really, Parke, what the hell ARE you doing on that boat for this guy to talk about you like that?

Your behavior has allowed people to openly mock me and shows a complete lack of respect. You seriously have zero respect for me. And I'm the laughing stock of random people who half-know me. You could have had all the fun in the world with anyone you wanted and have told them, "you know what, I had a girlfriend, she's in LA, she's a nice girl, but we've been having some problems and we're on a break and allowed to do stuff." And you could have been discreet. Instead, you choose to completely erase me from your life and present yourself as a completely single and available person. I really don't see how you thought this benefits you. Did you think it will reduce your chances if you tell people the truth? That you are on a break from a girl you still love and loves you?

Once again, I know that you ARE single and so am I, but I also know that you know perfectly well what I'm getting at. I'm trying not to get too hurt by this, because at the end of the day this public display of availability and promiscuity doesn't diminish me as much as it diminishes you. I think that your behavior has dragged our relationship through the mud, but it reflects more on you than it does on me. We had our issues before, but they were internal. You have taken them outside and hung them out for everyone to see. It's not my problem. But it's also not how I want to lead my life. It's disgusting.

Unfortunately I don't feel like I'm getting anything from you that makes me want to be associated with you in any way anymore. I don't feel any protection or love from your part. I don't feel that you want to be in a relationship with me and I'm not sure you want to be in a relationship with anyone. In fact, with your behavior people drop their jaws at the suggestion that you might be in a relationship. They find it unbelievable. I don't think anything is going to change any time soon.

I don't want to make any big statements or accusations or whatever, every story has two sides, but I never knew you were the person you have turned out to be.

Take good care of yourself.'

25

On this Saturday afternoon Valerie's on the phone telling me that Saul is on his way there and insisting that I go over to meet him. I'm sitting at home watching a movie called *Smother* about a 45-year-old woman in middle-of-nowhere southern California, who's trapped in an insipid marriage that's failed to give her any children and consequently develops an unhealthy co-dependence relationship with a desolate gay teen whom she meets in her local high school, where she works part-time as a janitor. This is part of Hallmark channel's Dangerous Minds weekend, two full days of TV movies examining psychotic behavior amongst the rural underclasses, a genre that's very specific but much richer and more enthralling than I ever had imagined. So I kinda don't want to go anywhere.

'You have to come over, please,' she says.

'Um, why?'

'You're going to love him. Saul is an awesome human being. He's so… spiritual and wise.'

That's a unique way to describe your pimp, I'm thinking.

'Besides, he really wants to meet you,' she adds.

'Why, does he want to have his aura challenged?'

'No. I just spent the afternoon with him and we talked a lot about you. I think you're really going to like him.'

'But I'm watching a movie right now. Can I come over after that's finished?'

She says yes and we hang up and I don't know exactly how I managed to get involved with another girl who's trying to make me do things that I don't want to, but perhaps that's every girl out there, or perhaps this is normal and I just can't deal with it because I have the same relationship skills and tolerance as both of my parents.

When I get to Sausalito the whole household is gathered around one of the kitchen tables shooting the breeze. Naturally, everyone is off their face. Saul's spirituality extends further than offering young people accommodation on his boat and creating an environment where they can fix their qi with long meditation sessions. An added very important element of this living arrangement is the generous supply of free drugs. Not the usual social drugs that people take at parties in LA, but particularly solipsistic, mind-altering ones like acid and magic mushrooms and ketamine. These kids really like to escape.

Saul is the only person here that I haven't met before. Valerie makes the introduction by jumping on me and wrapping her arms around my neck and her legs around my waist, and Saul also greets me very enthusiastically, although thankfully with less body contact. I have to admit, I'm disappointed to see that he's not physically what I expected. He's just a normal, slightly chubby Latin guy in his late 30s. I think I may have been watching too many Hallmark movies, where you can tell who the bad guy is as soon as he steps into the screen with his shady eyes, facial scar, thinning ponytail, and a raspy whisper. Saul has none of these, although he does have an unnaturally round little head leading directly from his double chin to his chest without bothering with a neck, and a nose that starts off heading right from the top of its bridge, then takes a sudden turn to the left, before ending up facing right again on its tip, managing to face three different directions all at once. Still, these are not TV movie criminal features to me.

I end up only staying for less than an hour. Saul may not physically be the cartoonish villain I wanted him to be, but observing his behavior around these hapless, lost kids makes me really uncomfortable. He has this weird power over them, a sense of control that's quite menacing. It's definitely an exchange of sorts; I don't doubt that they're getting something out of it: free accommodation, free food, drugs, whatever. And perhaps I would be more accepting of the circumstances if I were also part of that cycle. But that's exactly what I find distressing – how did these boys and girls, all around my age, find themselves in a situation where they want to do this? Where their life choice for their late teens / early 20s is to stay on some rich, creepy guy's boat and spend their days getting wasted and numbing their brains? I guess I'd be closer to an answer if I knew anything about these kids' backgrounds. Where they came from, who let them down, who wasn't there for them, who fucked them over. Of course, I don't care enough to do that. Not for them, not even for Valerie.

After half an hour, all I want to do is get out of there. I try to come up with an excuse, although I soon realize that's completely redundant.

'If anyone wants to pull out any of my teeth, I'm ready,' announces Sammy, the 19-year-old guy who's been living on the boat with his girlfriend for the last year or so, and it becomes obvious that the evening has lost direction so much that no one's going to care what I say or do.

Still, out of politeness, I ask Valerie if she wants to come have dinner with me, but she's shockingly not hungry after all those drugs and I just walk out on my own. I end up eating alone at this seafood restaurant by the Sausalito Yacht Club overlooking the bay and, in what's becoming a regular occurrence once again, missing Ryan.

We started talking a few days after I broke up with her. We've exchanged a couple of messages a week since then, and they've been kinda low key and sweet, making me think, well, maybe there's some life left in this yet.

Having nothing to do and no one to talk to, I take my phone out and read her last email to me, sent four days ago. I haven't written back to her yet.

'I have to send another email.

I've had the time to process what we discussed recently. I think you've got a right, mature approach towards this. I have to apologize for not reacting well to the whole break up. You have to remember that I'm very sensitive, which I think is a result of everything I went through with Trevor (although that's obviously not your fault and you shouldn't deal with its consequences). Thank you for being a grown up in this. I think your approach is wise, Parke. I really do. I often called you immature, but in this case I'm the one acting that way.

I'm OK with our break and with the "seeing other people" thing. I think this is a very sore point, because I'm sensationally insecure. It will be hurtful, but I think it's a learning curve. I need to be able to deal with this better now, while we're not together. I know that I shouldn't get so effected (*sic*) by it, especially as I can go and do the exact same thing. It's almost dumb to get so hurt by you kissing or having sex with someone else, if I'm also allowed to do the same thing (and knowing that I wouldn't be doing it to hurt you and it wouldn't take away from my love and how much I care for you).

I actually reckon you must get equally uncomfortable about any thoughts of me doing stuff with another guy, but I think the difference is that you probably have the ability to stop yourself from these thoughts being very detailed. Me, with my mind working at its regular pace, well … I can drive myself crazy.

You also have the strength to stop yourself from asking questions. I think this is wise. Like, when I told you that I did stuff with that person last week, you didn't question who it was, what we did exactly, where it was, etc. I think if you had (like I do) you would have upset yourself too.

So I don't know what the best policy is, really. We clearly still talk and message quite regularly, so I have the sense that when you do something with someone I will know and I will start the over thinking process I mentioned above. One idea would be to NOT be in touch at all until you come back, but I actually don't want to suggest that because I like talking to you. I don't want it to change. Even if we're not together, you're still my best friend. And I don't want to stop talking to my best friend. So I don't know. Do you have any ideas on this?

Again, you're single now and you can do as you wish, but I'm just putting across my feeling here (which may or may not be justified). I'm not saying things should be different.

Erm, these are all my thoughts. As you probably realize there isn't that much point in this, it's just random thoughts about the "being single" stuff, but I thought I'd share them. Because I like talking to you.

Would you mind writing a reply (or we can do Skype or something) just so I see how you are dealing with the whole thing. You know that this is my weakness and I could use some tips.'

When I go home after dinner, I'm too tired to write back a really lengthy response, but I do want to show some sense of goodwill on my part and send her a couple of paragraphs. I ask her not to worry about all the other people that we end up meeting this summer, I say that this is all inconsequential and suggest that perhaps when I'm back in Los Angeles we should see each other casually, maybe go on a few dates or something, and see how things feel between us.

She writes back within the half hour that it takes me to fall asleep:

'I think that dating again on a trial basis is a really great idea. I would kick myself if we couldn't make this work. I know that we both want it. Have a good night. You are my world.'

26

This is a Thursday a couple of weeks later, and on this Thursday I take Valerie out for late lunch, even though this relationship has now crossed over to the point where my level of enjoyment of being around her is only a tiny fraction of how annoying I find her. There is only so much free-spirited hippy shit one can take in exchange for a bit of venturous sex. Also, I'm bored of the sex.

We're having sushi at this place in Hayes Valley, which is pretty good despite catering mostly to workers on their lunch break and having a distinct fast food feel. I'm mostly, if not exclusively, focusing on uncovering the picture of the soccer player printed at the bottom of my Omega 3 Supreme sushi box, by methodically lifting small pieces of salmon, crab, rice and herb salad, whilst attempting to tune out Valerie. I believe she's going on about something relating to meditation or going to Burning Man or life-changing group sex experiences in lakes in Utah under the moonlight, or something along those lines anyway; I'm mostly guessing here, to be honest.

I start paying attention to her when I realize she's stopped talked for a minute or so. I look up and see that she's staring into her teriyaki chicken udon noodles and broth with a solemnity I haven't encountered in her face since I lost her in that k-hole on the boat a few weeks ago.

'What's up?' I ask.

'I'm just thinking,' she says, keeping the same fixed stare.

'Once upon a time people hunted, trekking for weeks in search of nourishment. They used to hunt and gather their food.'

'Oh yeah, I remember those days.'

She finally looks up.

'Now… we have this. Fish sliced into bite-sized portions and processed rice in little carton boxes.'

'You can still go hunting and gathering, if you like. I mean, agriculturally you're quite skilled already, what with your marijuana plant involvement.'

'Yes, there is that. Anyway, do you have any plans after this? Do you want to come with me and do something?'

No, not at all. 'Sure,' I say.

We drive east taking the I-80 over to Oakland, which is somewhere I really don't want to be right now.

'Would you like to tell me where we're going?' I ask.

'My father's house.'

'Oh.'

Sensing my gathering panic, she adds: 'Don't worry, he's not there. I just have to do something.'

I don't want to ask what that something is, but if I were to guess, and I am, I would think it involves stealing some cash from him, stealing his stash, or maybe some sort of revenge via arson. Something hotheaded and illegal, anyway. As I sit there getting worried about my own criminal implication in this endeavor, we drive through several West Oakland neighborhoods that I never want to see again and finally arrive at a small, two-storey house with a charcoal wood siding exterior. The only thing that anyone needs to know about this house and the street that we're on is that two doors down someone is having a sidewalk sale, and I mean sidewalk sale, not garage or yard sale (as there is neither). Sidewalk.

When we go in, Valerie grabs a giant trash bag and starts getting rid of things left, right, and centre. The place looks quite abandoned, not from a long time ago or anything, but as if somebody evacuated it suddenly maybe a week ago and hasn't been back since. I ask if I can help and she says no, she just needs to throw some stuff out and we can go.

I'm not particularly proud of my observation skills, but you'd have to be blind not to see that what we're doing is eliminating the traces of a former female presence in the house. Into the bag go scented candles, decorative wreaths, and various Christmas-themed knickknacks (this makes me wonder whether this woman got into the Hallmark channel's 'Christmas in June' special as much I did, and I conclude that she might have had if this house had cable, which I doubt). From the bathroom we throw out generic brand bath creams, fruity scrubs and shampoos for dry, damaged, or dyed hair (the woman is artificially blonde).

Valerie finally decides to reveal that we're here to move her dad's ex girlfriend out. Well, she moved out quite hastily a few days ago after a final big fight just picking up all her clothes and leaving, but all other evidence of her living in the house for the last six months are still around and her dad can't bear to look at it, because he's so mad at her. So he asked Valerie to come around and clear it out. This is quite fucked up as a situation, but who am I to pass judgment on people's maladjusted family circumstances after all, so I let this one go. I finally give her a helping hand to clear the kitchen area, an activity that peaks at the tragicomic moment when Valerie holds up a can of spray whipped cream and exclaims 'he gave that bitch everything', and I'm pretty sure she's not even being ironic.

I drive her back to Sausalito mostly in silence. She's still angry at the ex girlfriend and god knows what the whole story is there, but at the end of the day I'm not interested to find out, I don't care enough about Valerie's life to enquire or even console her. At the end of the day I'm definitely kinda over it.

When I get back home, I get changed and rush to the outdoor pool to have a quick swim before the sun goes down. I ask Denning to serve me an elaborate dinner for one completely unnecessarily in the dining room just to eradicate any memories of Valerie's dad's house in West Oakland and finally end up falling asleep on the sofa in the main living room, whilst playing on my laptop.

I know I can't have been laying there for too long when I get woken up by several abrupt tugs on my shirtsleeve. My mother is sitting on the coffee table opposite me. Impressively, and despite her current state, she's managing to maintain a perfect, upright posture. Still, her eyes are heavy and lost. Whatever little focus she's managing to sustain at the moment, she's directing it all intently at my face. I can't imagine this is going anywhere good.

'I haven't seen you in days,' she says.

'I've been out seeing friends a lot.'

She attempts to nod, causing her to drop her stare from my eyes onto the floor. With her eyes no longer fixed at me, I'm immediately more at ease.

'Is that girl here?'

'What girl?'

'The girl you've been seeing.'

'I'm not seeing anyone at the moment.'

She looks despondent, as if I keep letting her down with my lies.

'Fine. All I'm saying is you should spend some more time with your mother while you're here.'

'Yeah, maybe.'

As soon as I've said it though, I decide that I'm bored of this. I sit up to face her and add:

'Actually, I'm not sure that I want to. You are in the worst state that I've ever seen you.'

She gasps in mock offense and whispers in an unsteady tone:

'This is one of the most extraordinary allegations of all time.'

Seeing that we're not ready to go past amateur dramatics, I give up and start playing with my phone. She stays there sitting on the coffee table taking sips from her glass for several minutes before deciding to go on:

'I don't want us to fight.'

She puts her drink down, raises her hand and runs it down the opening of my shirt, stopping at the top button that's done up about halfway down my chest. I quickly stand up and start walking away from her. With a sudden spurt of energy she manages to come after me and grab my arm to turn me around.

'Where are you going?' she says.

'You need help. Serious, serious help.'

'What the hell do you mean?' she says. 'You can't talk to me like that.'

'You're a complete mess. You have got to stop. Just stop. I hate you. I can't remember a time when I didn't hate you.'

She takes a swing at me, aiming for my face, but it's very sluggish and I grab hold of her wrist mid-air and try to force her back. This causes her to lose her balance and fall backwards on the wooden floor. It looks painful, not that I care.

It takes her a moment to get her bearings. When she does, she looks up and fixes her eyes on mine once again. They are bloodshot and tired, but there's a purpose behind there now. She takes a deep breath, cracks a smile and shouts two words loudly, viciously, with perfect clarity and control:

'Mother. Fucker.'

I turn around and walk away, leaving her there on the floor.

27

Back in my room, I start going through emails that Ryan has sent me over the summer. Thousands and thousands of words, some of which I haven't even read, most of which I definitely haven't paid attention to. There's a message that was sent about a week after I broke up with her, which I certainly haven't seen before, where she goes on to list dozens of memories from things we did together over the last year and a half. She wants to remember only the good points now that it's over, she says, life's too short and painful to hang on to bad memories. She ends the message with this:

'I know that I've listed all these fun memories above, but what I will keep the most, is the fact that for a considerable amount of time, your very existence made me happy.'

I don't know. Overall this sounds forced and corny to me, but right now I'm willing to take it.

It's nearly 11pm, which means that Markus must be sitting at home getting stoned with nothing to do, so I give him a call on Skype. Markus is sitting at home getting stoned with nothing to do.

''Sup, home slice?' he says.

'Oh. I see. Nothing much. What are you up to?'

'Just finished watching a movie. Planning my next move.'

'Good for you. What was the movie?'

'You know. Some dumb, mass destruction, post-apocalyptic thing.'

'Nice. Reminds me of how things are here with my mother.'

'Are things post-apocalyptic in Hillsborough?'

'Yes. But only emotionally.'

'What did she do now?'

'You know. The usual.'

'Well, don't let it bother you. It takes all sorts.'

'OK. Whatever that means. Listen, I think I'm going to come back soon.'

'I like the sound of that.'

'Plus, I'm also thinking that maybe I want to try things out with Ryan again.'

'Why? Did you fall back in love with each other?'

'It's not that we had fallen out of love. It's just that she couldn't stand the person that I am and I couldn't deal with that.'

'And are you different person now? One that she'll be able to stand?'

'Slightly. Also, we've talked a lot and she promises that she really sees things differently now. Also also, I'm starting to think that there isn't much better out there.'

'This all sounds very promising. I have high hopes for this and I can't wait for all the future Thanksgivings I will be invited to when the two of you have settled down on her meat farm in Albuquerque.'

'I know, right? Anyway, it's not like I come back and we'll immediately get back together. We're planning to casually date for a bit. See how things work out.'

'So sensible.'

'In fact, I was thinking that perhaps we could start completely from scratch. Maybe role-play or something. You know, go to a bar or a club separately, pretend to meet there and pick each other up.'

'You should definitely do that. It's very "55-year-old couple in desperate need of reigniting the flame". Next you can take a Caribbean cruise or perhaps a pottery class together on Friday nights. I would love to see how this works though. I'd be interested in coming to watch. Do you have any ideas where you'll get to accidentally bump into each other first?'

'I don't know. It's to be decided. What advice would you give me on how to play this? You sound like you definitely have some.'

'While I have never gone somewhere and pretended I didn't know someone I actually know for the thrill of "meeting" them, I have gone many places and pretended I didn't know someone I actually knew, and I have gone to many places and met people I didn't know, so I guess you could say I have some experience in this.'

'Sounds perfect. Give me some hard and fast rules.'

He lights up a new joint, takes a few drags and says:

'1. Do not use fake names.

2. Try to wear something new. New clothing, or new bag for her; not a wig or new piercing.

3. Avoid making the mistake of starting the conversation with "Why were you late?" or "Remember that time…"

4. Do not tell friends or acquaintances the time and location of your meeting, unless they live in a different country or are in prison or could not possibly show up. Apart from me. You can tell me, obviously.

5. If you happen to accidentally see someone you know during this meeting, do *not* tell them what you are actually doing.

There. This should get you started. Can I go make some popcorn now?'

'Yes, this has been extremely helpful, as always, thanks. Enjoy your popcorn.'

'Wait, when are you coming back then?'

'Maybe in a week or so. Maybe sooner.'

It ends up being sooner, because on Friday morning I get an email from Neon Sphere, asking me if I'd be interested in going back there to do some freelance work again. Not that this makes any sense whatsoever, but they've laid off so many people that there just isn't enough staff around to get the work done. So they thought of me. This has even been signed off by Rothchild himself, even though he doesn't quite know that the freelancer my former line manager has decided to contact and rehire is me. I think that we're all getting a perverse sense of satisfaction from this.

This job offer gives me the excuse that I needed to get the hell out of San Francisco as quickly as possible, and a quick thirty-six hours later I'm sitting back in my apartment in LA with Markus going through Facebook invites trying to choose which party to go to. In another day and a half, my life has reverted to revolving around exchanging hilarious emails, participating in office-based scheming and plotting, and grossly exaggerating the importance of my relationships with my colleagues, just to make the working day go quicker. This isn't progress, I'm sure of it, there's no advancement, but it's somewhat comforting being back here doing something so casual and familiar, even with the minuscule fulfillment it provides.

Then I get an email from Rich Cerna that says 'welcome back, did you happen to bring a tall tree and a short piece of rope with you?' and I kinda think that perhaps 'minuscule' might even be an embellishment of the level of fulfillment that the average person gets from his office job.

I'm not really in the mood to get depressed on my first day back at work though, so I ignore Rich and his suicidal tendencies and send an email to Kurt Morency who, I should hope, continues to alleviate his boredom with sexual delusions and affairs he's dreamt up instead. Because nothing ever changes, least of all people, Kurt is most definitely still caught up in the laughable cliché that he's created for himself.

'Have you seen the new temp in reception yet? HAWT, Filipino, early 20s. That's all I can tell you for now. More details after I've taken her out for lunch or fucked her in the handicapped restroom, whichever happens first.'

'Is she handicapped?'

'No. Just more space there.'

'I see. The sex you are planning must be very acrobatic. Why do we need a reception temp anyway? Where's Kwasi?'

'They let Kwasi go. So now we just have this temp on Monday and Tuesday mornings, another temp called Hildur (Icelandic, not my type, still would) on Wednesday and Thursday mornings, and nobody answering phone calls or letting people in on Monday, Tuesday, Wednesday and Thursday afternoons and during the whole of Fridays.'

'It sounds like a very effective system, well done.'

'Thank you. Now go and see the temp. Her name is either Maria or Leilani, I can't remember which one right now. Maybe both. I do remember that she has a very sexy manner, bohemian outlook (she told me she moved apartments by doing five round trips on the bus) and a dazzling smile.'

'I find it interesting how you interpret "impoverished ethnic minority who moves house on the bus" into "bohemian outlook". You must really like this girl.'

'Er…how many racist assumptions here? She may be half Filipino, but definitely not impoverished and I think she's in college.'

'Even so, I still don't know how to defend a 20-something college girl from Los Angeles who moves her possessions on the bus. I can only put it down to genetic thriftiness (via third world sensibilities). Does she also not have a handbag and carry all her stuff in a bamboo basket that she balances on her head?'

'Jesus Christ.'

'Ugh, I'm only joking.'

'OK. Well, since you refuse to stand up and go see her for yourself, here are some pictures I found on her Facebook.'

Five or six emails later with pictures of Maria / Leilani in seductive bikini poses sipping colorful cocktails at various beach bars across the Californian coast, and conscious of the looks I've been getting from people walking past my desk, I write back:

'Stop sending me these pictures, you maniac.'

'Are they turning you on?'

'Yes, and everyone else around me.'

Then Kurt stops sending me these pictures, then Rothchild walks in to the office, takes a look in my direction and raises his eyebrows in a mixture of shock, disbelief and disgust, and then I go out to get some lunch.

28

On Tuesday evening, Ryan and I have our so-called first date. This is a unique situation, as she still has a key to my place plus a lot of her stuff over there, not to mention that she's already spent the night since I came back, but I'm sure in some other dimension, on some planet somewhere, this relationship trial thing is valid and useful and not just a ridiculous story we keep telling ourselves.

During this dinner date, Ryan tells me that she missed me so much over the summer, and despite spending *some* time being very angry at me and thinking that I'm a parasitic fuck and very selfish and generally a massive waste of human life, she also spent quite a lot of time thinking that she can't be without me, it's all her fault, I am who I am, I don't have to change anything and she's happy to accept me that way. This is nothing more than a succinct summary of several thousand words sent in a few dozen emails over the last few months, but I finally take the opportunity to accept the apology she's been offering since I went away, and I think that by the end of the meal we're officially back together.

I seal the deal by sharing my theory that we might not be perfect for each other, but at the end of the day you have to draw the line somewhere, get off the carousel and spend the rest of your life with whichever partner you are with at that point. We have our first argument since we got back together a few minutes ago over how crass or romantic this sounds (she says crass, I say romantic). I pay the bill and we go home to consummate our reinstated relationship with a satisfying fuck on the conjugal bed.

On Wednesday morning I get up early, at the same time as Ryan, and I go to work, because I guess this is what I do now. At work, I'm surprised to see that another person with a sudden professional conscience who now turns up on time is Theo Rothchild. Now, if I were I different person, one who worries more, I suppose I'd be thinking that he's there to spy on me, possibly create a hostile working environment, maybe make me quit this job by his mere presence, but I try to maintain good faith in people, plus

I'm usually quite oblivious to their motivations (through a complete lack of interest) so I don't read to much into it for now.

I do start to read quite a lot into it about an hour later, after Rothchild has sat there and subjected me to a series of disapproving sideways glances interspersed with the occasional explicitly antagonistic glare. I decide to take a break from the group email conversation that I'm part of, where eight of my colleagues are exchanging stories depicting how laughable Rothchild is, and walk over to the kitchen to get myself a drink. When I'm back at my desk, I open up a storyboard for a strategy game called Dark Ages II that I need to be working on and sit back on my chair, thinking of where I can take it next.

Rothchild takes a spiteful look at me and says:

'Are you getting a lot done sitting there with your arms crossed?'

Not even that shocked, I reply:

'I'm thinking.'

'Yeah,' he says, which seems like a complete non sequitur, but he is an idiot after all.

'I don't have to keep clicking buttons or pressing keys like a trained monkey to convince you that I'm working.'

Then I laugh pleasantly to pretend that this was a joke, then he does the same because he doesn't really have another option other than to take this as a joke and then I get up and head out for lunch, even though it's before 10.30am.

When I come back an hour later, Rothchild is gone, so I'm left to work on my storyboard uninterrupted.

Later in the afternoon, I find a message from Kurt in my junk mail folder. Kurt has written:

'I have thought very long and hard about this and my favorite Neon Sphere person is Hildur, the Wednesday / Thursday reception temp.

I like the following things about her:

a) Her accent reminds me of Björk. Björk is my favorite singer of all time and I just want Hildur to recite Björk lyrics to me, maybe even the spoken word intro from the Bachelorette video

b) Her name is a combination of Hilda and Hitler

c) Her spoken English is even worse than Kwasi's, and there's something very comforting about that. I mean if people like that can get jobs, surely I'm going to be employed for life

That's it.'
I reply:

'a) Sorry for the delay. For some reason your email arrived in my junk folder
'b) Yes, Hildur seems nice. I just had to make a conference call from the room that's facing her desk and she did spend the entire forty-five minutes I was there rocking on her chair whilst listening to music, which in turn gave me a sense of nausea and made me feel disorientated, but that was only mildly annoying
c) Who's "Björk"?'

And then it's time to go home, or not far off anyway, so I just leave.

On the way home I'm listening to NPR, and that is most definitely not my choice, I've never tuned into this station, but that's what you get when you frequently drive in a car with Ryan. Some actor is on, giving a very humble interview about his latest film and the Oscar buzz surrounding his name, before revealing that he never smiles in photo shoots anymore, because he knows that if he smiles once, that's the picture they're going to use. I take it that's a terrible thing, although we're never given any further clues as to why.

Then the interviewer, a haggard-voiced pseudo-intellectual who's spent the entirety of the broadcast fawning over him, leads the actor to discuss the recent death of his father from cancer, and the actor takes his cue to emote and let us know that this was a pivotal moment for him, a life changing event that shifted his whole perception of the world with immediate effect from the moment the father left his last breath. It all became clear, apparently, most things in life are not that important and we can't waste our time stressing about them, but you only get to realize that when something really bad happens.

This guy must have had a really tough life when that revelatory moment, that epiphany about what is and what isn't important in life comes to you when you're nearly 40 and the worst thing that's happened to you is the loss of a parent. And yes, the actor is 38; I ask my phone halfway through the interview to confirm. Honestly, these people make mine and Markus' lives seem tortured.

When I get home, Markus is sitting in his living room getting stoned with a guest. I've never met or even seen this person before. He's introduced to me as Anthony, pronounced in a very British way. I don't know if Anthony is British or not, because he doesn't actually say anything to me. I believe his tolerance to industrial strength pot must be lower than Markus', so he's sunk into a mild coma. Anthony's quite short, maybe around 5'9", unnaturally muscular, with a marine haircut and covered in badass tattoos. This means that he's either a marine or that he's gay. He's only wearing a pair of shorts and a backward 59FIFTY fitted cap. This means that he's gay. I'm sure I should find this scene more unsettling than I do, but, really, what kind of an idiot would I have to be to be surprised by any of this?

'What's going on over here?' I ask.

'We're just hanging,' Markus replies.

'Good for you. Who's Anthony? I doubt Anthony can hear us right now, can he?'

Markus glances at him.

'No, I doubt it. He's just a kid. He's cool though. I met him at Party Boy Michael Murphy's house last night.'

'Was Michael Murphy having a party?'

'Michael Murphy was having a party.'

'What's Anthony's story?'

'I don't know that much. He's just moved here. He hasn't got anywhere to stay, so I told him he can crash here for a while, if he wants.'

'All right then. What's new online?'

He takes a look at the iPad that he's holding in front of him and says:

'As I'm sure you know, Rae and Tommy's wedding is in a couple of weeks. Are you going?'

'I'm going.'

'Well, Rae is going wedding crazy on Facebook, Twitter, and Instagram, but mainly Pinterest.'

'And why are you following Rae Prinz on Facebook, Twitter, Instagram, and Pinterest?'

'I don't know, what else is there to do?'

'I guess not much.'

'Oh I'll tell you what I've realized I hate having spent the last few hours online though.'

'Do you really need more things to hate?'

'Yes, definitely need this one. Right, you know what's really cool right now? If you're white, you have to talk about white people as if you're non-white.'

'What do you mean?'

'Well, you know. You have to be dismissive of aspects of your own culture, pretending that you're black or something.'

'Examples?'

'Like, when people say "music white people like". Or that somebody "dances like a white person". When they're white themselves. You know, pretending that they've reached a level of multiculturalism and open-mindedness that the rest of us can only dream of.'

'I don't know, Markus. I think you only hate that because you're racist.'

Anthony, who must be able to hear us after all, sniggers, although he keeps his eyes closed still and doesn't move from his 45-degree angle on the couch.

'Why are you laughing?' Markus says playfully. 'I've just been accused of being racist.'

'Not for the first time I imagine,' Anthony says in British accent, maintaining his stupor.

'Kid's got your number,' I tell Markus, because it seems like an aloof, amiable sort of statement that tactfully indicates support of whatever the hell is going on between them, and go next door to my apartment to have dinner.

29

'It's Ryan's birthday the day after Rae and Tommy's wedding,' I tell Markus.

'Yes, I know, I have Facebook too. Does the wedding get in the way of your plans for her birthday?'

'We don't have any plans, so I'm going to say no.'

'Don't you think you should make some plans?'

'I guess so. Maybe I should propose to her or something. Girls like that, right?'

'Yes, do that. What a marvelous idea. Let's see if this is the right time though – how old is she turning?'

'Um, 29, I think.'

'Whoa. Yes, a proposal would be age appropriate. And how long have you been going out?'

'Well, it feels to me that it's been longer than twenty-nine years, possibly forty or more, but this doesn't seem possible mathematically...'

'... *if* she's given you her real age.'

'You're right, assuming she's given me her real age, which is very questionable anyway.'

'So you're going to propose, it's settled. And are you really going to marry her?'

'I don't know, one step at a time. Let's go buy a ring or something.'

'I'm not going anywhere right now. Anthony's on his way over here. Shouldn't you be at work anyway? I thought that's something you did now.'

'Yeah, I thought that's something I did now too, but it turns out it's much easier staying at home and occasionally working from here. So I've reverted to that.'

When Anthony turns up, I leave them alone and go back to my apartment where I spend the next four hours finishing a game storyboard I've been working on for Neon Sphere and looking at wedding rings online. I send the finished draft of the storyboard over to my team after

6pm and just a few minutes later I get an email back from Rothchild, who wasn't even copied in on my original message. Given that his role is very managerial, broad and unidentified, he doesn't really have any involvement in individual projects, and he couldn't possibly tell you what any of the game designers are working on at any given point, this sudden hands on involvement is very peculiar indeed. What does he know about the game I'm working on? How is he aware that I even sent this email just now? Everyone in the office hates him too much to have told him anything, so the only logical explanation is that he has nothing better to do than track everyone's email and read our messages to each other. And on this Wednesday evening, he has this to say to me:

'Parke,
Thank you for sending through the draft storyboard for Exit Through The Wound. Were you in the office today? How many hours did you work on this?
Best regards,
Theo.'

I reply:

'Theo,
I wasn't in the office today; I was working from home. I've been working on the storyboard for the last couple of days, so approximately fifteen hours in total.
Parke.'

'Parke,
Following the recent review of our contractor regulations, which you should be aware of, all contractors/freelancers must be present in the office for the hours they bill Neon Sphere. Remote working is no longer allowed for temporary members of staff. Therefore, if you would like to continue working for Neon Sphere, you are required to do so from our premises here.
Best regards,
Theo.'

I write back:

'What difference does it make?'

'Parke,
There is no way of tracking contractors' hours unless they are present here. Neon Sphere can no longer authorize payment without proof of the hours worked.
Best regards,
Theo.'

Primarily because his default signature of 'best regards' is really starting to get to me (I really doubt he's wishing me the best of anything right now, let alone his regards) I open up Paintbrush and make a basic line drawing of a stick figure sitting at a desk in front of a computer screen using terrible, shaky black lines on a white background. Above the desk I draw a wall calendar and a big, round clock with the hands showing 9.30am. I save the picture and replicate it, just changing the time to 5.30pm.

In my next email to Theo, I write:

'Theo,
I completely understand where you're coming from. It would be very presumptuous of me to expect payment without having provided solid proof of the hours I've worked. Luckily, I have surveillance cameras installed in my apartment and can provide still images of me sitting at my desk first thing this morning, and right at the very end of my day. I'm attaching them here. Please note the time on the clock on my wall. You will see that I literally haven't moved from my desk between 9.30am and 5.30pm today. I trust this is sufficient supporting evidence for the timesheets and invoice I will provide at the end of the month. If you have any further questions, please let me know.
Best regards,
Parke.'

I send the email off with the two attachments and go outside for a swim. I suppose that's where this story ends.

On Wednesday of the following week, the day before we're all supposed to travel up to Palo Alto for Tommy and Rae's Friday wedding, I get up, have breakfast, and go out to buy an engagement ring for Ryan. When that's done, I come home and go straight to Markus'. That kid, Anthony, has been staying there full-time. He's now even coming to the wedding as his plus one.

'Look,' Markus says. They're both highly entertained by this. Anthony's in stitches. 'We got a birthday card for Ryan.'

He hands me a white, square card with an illustration of two eggs on the front. The eggs have faces drawn on them and are both wearing party hats. One is cracked, lying sideways on a kitchen counter with its yolk pouring out. Its face is one of complete agony. There's a little bicycle next to it, which is also sideways with a bent front wheel. I believe the premise is that the cracked egg had a cycling accident, perhaps on his way to a third egg's birthday party. The other egg is looking over in despair. A tagline underneath reads: 'Have a cracking birthday'.

Inside, Anthony – it's a handwriting I don't recognize, so I assume it's his – has written:

'Happy Birthday, Ryan. I chose this card, because it's the first one that jumped out at me. It depicts two eggs. The female one is called Meg and the male one is called Beg (he's into role play). Anyway, I suppose I should wrap this up now. Love, Anthony and Markus.'

I hand the card back to Markus. I don't get this. None of it is funny. It also bothers me that Anthony's written the message, has signed his name first and has included the word 'love'. He barely knows Ryan; I think they've met maybe once, just in passing, over the last week. The whole thing strikes me as very odd. Very intrusive. And these jokes that I'm not in on…what's happening to Markus?

Perhaps sensing my growing aversion to him, Anthony decides to make himself scarce by going to the gym.

'I need to be half a stone musclier,' he says, whatever the hell that means.

'And four shades less pale…' he adds after catching his reflection in the mirror on the way out.

'Yes, but not everywhere,' says Markus with very specific intent, right before Anthony walks out the door.

'You were talking about his ass, weren't you?'

'I was talking about his ass.'

'Thanks for that. What's the deal with this kid, anyway? I'll be honest with you, Markus. I'm not a big fan.'

'There's no deal. I guess he can be a bit obnoxious at times. The thing with Anthony is, he needs a good, hard pounding. Luckily, it's also what he wants. So it works out well for all parties involved.'

'Is that all there is to it?'

'Yes, I think so.'

'But in the meantime he lives here? And you're happy to bring him along and introduce him to everyone at major social events, like the Palo Alto-based wedding of the year?'

'I don't know. I don't actually want him to come with.'

'Well, you shouldn't bring him then.'

'Maybe I won't.'

'Don't.'

'OK.'

30

Ryan has had the decency to take two sick days off work, so we get the chance to fly to San Francisco and drive down to Palo Alto by Thursday early evening. Despite being there in time for it, Ryan makes us skip the dinner Tommy and Rae have organized on the night before their wedding for the 'closest friends only' and insists that we spend the evening alone. This is not just their wedding weekend, I'm told; this is her birthday weekend too after all. On the one hand I'm not really dying to go to Tommy and Rae's dinner and most likely get propositioned to participate in some group sex scenario again like I did at their engagement party, but on the other hand I have to wonder how much this woman is going to milk her birthday.

I'm not really that familiar with Palo Alto and this is Ryan's first time here, so we drive around town to find somewhere to eat. A really old song comes on the radio – something about the singer's love for you still being strong, something about the boys of summer having gone – and Ryan jumps off her seat and turns the volume up really high.

'Oh my God,' she says. 'Do you know this song?'

'Kinda.'

'Oh come on. You don't know *any* songs.'

She sounds like she takes pleasure from this. She must consider it to be some sort of achievement being familiar with a few of songs from thirty-five years ago when she was a teenager.

'Did I never tell you this was my first ever favorite song?' she continues. 'I was a little kid. I was in my uncle's…'

'…pick-up truck on the way back from potato digging standing in the back screaming the words against the wind as he was shooting down the highway?'

She attempts to kill me with a sideways glance, doesn't finish her story and points at a pizza place that I'm driving past as her preferred venue for dinner. We go in, have pizza with about two dozen Stanford undergrads and head back to the hotel. The rest of the wedding party that falls under 'close friends' is also staying at this hotel and are also just making their way back. I stay out to have drinks in the bar with them, or watch them have drinks anyway, and Ryan goes to bed.

When I get a text right before 1am while I'm still out, I assume that it's Ryan asking me where I am and setting up a nice, huge fight for when I get back. Instead, it's from my mother.

'Honey make sure to watch Nightline on ABC. They had a feature on the church of Hallgrimur in Reykjavik. It will bring you to tears.'

Seconds later, she follows up with:

'You can find it online, can't you? I was sitting here watching it literally in tears.'

And:

'I miss you.'

Never one to shy away from high drama, I'm thinking. Although, I can actually picture her sitting there buzzed off her nut, sobbing away to whatever shit this is about some god damn church somewhere in Iceland.

I haven't heard from her and I haven't made an effort to contact her since that evening in Hillsborough. The last image I have is her collapsed on the floor, and the last word I've heard come out of her mouth is that thing that she called me. I want to leave it this way. I want to leave it this way so it's always clear to me who she is, what she's done to me, and how much I fucking hate her.

'Some people are not meant to have children', Ryan told me during one of our fights. My mother is *definitely* one of them.

I delete the messages and put the phone back in my pocket. People are starting to go to bed. I take a walk with Katie, stopping to quickly make out with her on the green between the parking lot and the back entrance of the hotel, and then go back to my room.

The next day, the actual wedding ceremony is mercifully short. The most laughable moment is when Tommy and Rae exchange their personalized vows, which must have unquestionably been Rae's idea. In hers, we find out that not only are they partners, but they're also best friends. This is a concept no one has ever come up with before. We also find out that they've never fought, never had an argument once in their lives. This is also a brand new notion, but purely because it's completely fabricated. Despite being trite and heavily romanticized, at least Rae's ideas are all her own. Tommy has handled this task simply by going online, typing 'personalized wedding vows' into Google and creating a montage of the various results. The outcome is a collection of vapid, generic statements going around in a meandering, seemingly endless cycle. First they're crossing a threshold together, then he gives her his soul, then he promises to always cherish her, and then we're back at the beginning, where they're entering a holy union, because, you know, she's every breath that he takes. This is followed by a brief religious segment by atheist Tommy, where we're told that he prayed for Rae before he ever met her, not to mention that she's the *answer* to every prayer he ever prayed. In delivering all this, Tommy has chosen to adopt a very concentrated, unblinking stare into Rae's eyes, designed to convey the sincerity of his feelings. To me, it reminds of the look a serial killer might fix a prostitute with while reciting his moralist manifesto right before strangling her. When his cut-and-paste vows namecheck the audience ('right in front of these loving people') he extends his left arm, while keeping the stare, and moves it backward to travel across the range of the guests, who are sitting there transfixed, lost in his magical words, recognizing all the quotes from somewhere, but not the person delivering them. This movement seems particularly unnatural as Tommy is right-handed and seems unable to perform the sweep in one smooth move, and I don't know why this bothers me so much, but it does.

Post-ceremony, everyone gets very drunk very quickly, which seems to be the only way either to sit through or deliver any of the speeches. Once again, being the only person on the premises with complete clarity of mind does me no favors. The best man, a nauseating goofy type with the mistaken self-impression of a raconteur, whom I've never seen before today, spends a good thirty minutes recollecting Stanford stories, including varsity stories, dorm shenanigans, and some crazy mishaps that took place in class. I'm starting to think he and Tommy met in college and that college was Stanford. The only useful outtake from this speech is that we now have an explanation as to why we had to decamp to Palo Alto for this event.

Then a series of relatives take turns on the mic and I've zoned out by this point to be honest, but the overall gist is that an unprecedented incidence has taken place here: the nicest guy on the planet has gone and found the nicest girl on the planet and they both lucked the fuck out because they're now here getting married.

I try to eye roll about all this with the other guests at my table, but none of them are having any of it. Ryan's pretending to feel unwell and doesn't want to hear any of my jokes and Markus is in a k-hole or some speed-induced journey of self-discovery or whatever (pretty unreachable right now in any case). The other people sitting with us are a cousin of Tommy's with his dull, grey wife, who turned up from some backwater town somewhere and decided only to talk to each other once they cast their eyes on Markus (ok, he is wearing sunglasses indoors and possibly drooling a little bit) and a friend of Rae's from college with her girlfriend. Both of them seem like quirky, girly lesbians who wear all the fashions but only in the way that suits them, only on their terms, and I don't actually want to get involved with either of them, because they intimidate me. This must be the worst put together wedding table ever.

When the speeches are over, we're free to leave the shackles of our mismatched tables and roam around the hotel function room. I stand up with Ryan and we walk to the edge of the dance floor. She appears to be in some sort of mood, but it's really quite difficult to tell anymore. When isn't she in a mood?

'Thank God,' I say.

'Thank God for what?'

'Thank God we could leave that table. Those people. Where did they find them?'

'You're judgmental, as always. I quite liked Harriet.'

'Who the hell is Harriet?'

'Tommy's cousin's wife. You just spent three hours sitting next to them.'

'Well, they didn't exactly make an effort to integrate. They took one look, and I'm sure they dismissed us before we dismissed them.'

'You know, Markus isn't the most relatable...'

'People like Markus a lot. What I find most interesting is that you always manage to bond with those types of people. The Harriet types. I don't understand what you like about them. I don't see what you have in common with them, why you want to be their friend and spend your time around them. People just like your ex boyfriend. With no prospects, nothing to look forward to, no desire whatsoever to be anyone or do anything of any substance. It's just such a sad, dreary life. What's the appeal?'

'What you don't realize, Parke, is that many, many people out there lead these "sad, dreary lives". In fact, most people do. Most people don't have your money, they don't have big houses, they're not even that good looking or whatever else you consider to be of substance. You're never exposed to anyone's real life though, outside your stupid little circle, and you don't know any of this. I'm not going to shut myself off from everyone whose existence you don't deem worthwhile.'

'But why? You don't have to be around them. You're not one of *those* people.'

'Well maybe I fucking am.'

'You really are not.'

She grunts, exasperated. 'I don't want to talk about this anymore. Just drop it. I've had a headache for the past two days that we've been here. You're just too much. I find it impossible to be around you. It feels like constantly having a weight on my chest and I can hardly breathe.'

'I'm confused,' I say. 'What hurts? Your chest or your head?'

She punches me hard on the leg.

'You know what, I'm going outside for a walk,' I say and limp away for effect.

I grab Markus who's standing a few feet away with a glass of Scotch in his hand looking spaced out, although noticeably more conscious than earlier, and step outside on to the stone-paved patio leading to the back garden.

'Well, we're arguing again. I'm hazardous to her health now too, apparently. I'm causing her a suspicious pain that's traveling between her head and her chest.'

'I really wouldn't worry about that. Imagine being her – her brain is likely so small that the pain she must feel has no choice but to have moved to her chest.'

I find this so utterly hilarious and let out an uproarious laugh.

While this happens, I turn around to catch my breath and see Ryan's shocked, flustered face. She's heard what he said and is starting to run away back into the main hall. I run after her. I grab her arm and she screams at me to leave her alone. Everyone's watching. I let her go. I see her making her way back to our room with tears in her eyes, and I go outside to find Markus.

'Fuck. Look what you did, you fucking idiot.'

'Oh, shut up. Nothing's happened. She'll have forgotten about it in ten minutes.'

'You're such a dick. How can you not care? We've really hurt her feelings.'

'I'm sorry I sound calm, I assure you I'm hysterical,' he says. He laughs and takes a swig from the bottle he's managed to get hold of.

'Fuck you,' I shout. 'You're a fucking mess.'

Some people have started to come outside. I can't deal with any of this. I want to be alone. I turn my back on Markus and start walking away from the building. He doesn't even make a pretense of following me, which really is for the best. I get to the end of the garden and sit down on a rusty, metal swing. The grass is wet here and my shoes are covered in mud. I get my phone out and attempt to call Ryan, but she doesn't pick up. It's ten minutes past midnight on the 4th of September. This is now officially her birthday.

I feel nothing inside me but hatred. I hate everything. I hate Markus, the mud on my shoes, the fact that I don't have a dozen relatives to tell everyone how great I am in their wedding speeches, and my mother. I hate Rae Prinz, the Brandts' 4th of July parties, how dark it is everywhere around me on this god damn swing, and Los Angeles. I hate my father, of course, Theo Rothchild, the four-poster bed I slept in whilst growing up, and every whore I've ever slept with. But above all I hate myself, because I'm such an ugly, ugly, hateful son of a bitch. An ugly, ugly, hateful motherfucker.

I'm currently under the impression that the one person in the world who can make me feel better is Ryan, and I guess I can't be sure until I go back in and hold her in my arms. I get up and walk through the garden back to the hotel. Avoiding the wedding reception, I go straight inside using the back door next to the parking lot.

In the elevator I check the time again. Ryan went back to the room just twenty minutes ago. I hope she's still there.

I walk into the room to find her rummaging through her purse with her back turned to me. There's a small pause – she's sensed that I've come back – but it's all too brief, she doesn't care enough to stop. She picks out a German target pistol, which I recognize from having belonged to my mother for years, most likely my grandfather before her, and turns around. The pistol is usually kept in a bureau in the study back at the Hillsborough house. It's old but it's oiled and functional and as far as I remember a box of shells is placed right next to it. I don't know when Ryan got hold of it, how long she's been carrying it around.

'Where did you get this?' I ask, pointlessly.

She remains quiet. She's holding the gun rather clumsily, as if she doesn't know how an object like this works, what exactly it's for. She's never looked younger to me than she does at this moment; she's almost childlike.

'What do you think you're doing?'

Her eyes are fixed on mine, heavy and blank, her mouth forming a faint smirk but refusing to answer me. Raising her right hand, she parts her lips, still remaining silent, and places the pistol inside her mouth pointing up. It seems so big compared to her features, inside her. The sight is grotesque. I get a stomach convulsion and close my eyes. I keep my eyes closed both through the loud bang and the thump of her slender body hitting the floor.

Acknowledgements

Mum and Dad for making sure that I'm never really scared of anything and I'll never depend on anyone. My sister for somehow believing that I'm better than I actually am. James and Andrea for picking up the fragments of my life, more or less, last summer. Carrie, the starting point for all my female leading characters. The gentleman who broke me down, because how can you possibly write when you've never been damaged? Llwyd always. Tim for reading the first draft and his American adaptations. Those kids in London who I met in the clubs and grew up with. Everyone who bought, read, or reviewed *Exit Through The Wound*. Everyone who still knows what London Preppy is, seven years later. Finally, Andre Labonte, Diamond Tokuda, Jonathan Hawkings, Kevin Lawlor, and Rommel Dorado for the support.

A Limehouse Books Publication

© North Morgan 2014

First published 18 September 2014.

Typset in Arno Pro, Arial and Futura.

Limehouse Books
Flat 30,
58 Glasshouse Fields
London
E1W 3AB

northmorgan.com

limehousebooks.co.uk

Printed at Grosvenor Group London.

Distributed in North America by SCB Distributors and in EU by Turnaround.